"It is time for that lesson now."

Manny was startled by his words. "What lesson?" she asked.

With incredible quickness Huw was behind her, turning her around to face him. "I'm going to teach you not to be afraid of men, Manny," he said. "Shall we start with...this?"

At once he was kissing her, light inconsequential kisses on her brows and then on each eyelid. Then she felt his warm breath close to her ear, and wondered why, when she so wholeheartedly disliked him, she was standing still like this waiting for another kiss. A kiss on her lips.

She heard him laughing softly, teasing her. "That's enough instruction for now. More lessons later," he promised. "Sleep now."

Manny watched him walk away. Sleep! How could she sleep when her mind was in such a whirl?

JOYCE DINGWELL
is also the author of these
Harlequin Romances

Many of these titles are available at your local bookseller.

For a free catalogue listing all available Harlequin Romances
and Harlequin Presents, send your name and address to:

HARLEQUIN READER SERVICE,
M.P.O. Box 707, Niagara Falls, NY 14302
Canadian address: Stratford, Ontario N5A 6W2

Come Back to Love

by

JOYCE DINGWELL

Harlequin Books

TORONTO • LONDON • LOS ANGELES • AMSTERDAM
SYDNEY • HAMBURG • PARIS • STOCKHOLM • ATHENS • TOKYO

Original hardcover edition published in 1980
by Mills & Boon Limited

ISBN 0-373-02402-9

Harlequin edition published May 1981

CHAPTER ONE

MANNY paused a quivering moment at the entrance of the hotel where she and her father had always stayed on their visits to Sydney, then took a deep steadying breath and walked in.

At once, as she had known it would, the past enfolded her. For eleven years the two Norberts, widowed artist Hal Norbert and daughter Emmanuelle, had spent their city breaks at Sydney's Hotel Southerly, enjoying the clamour and glamour after a lonely northern beach, trying out sophisticated restaurants, fitting in as many theatres as they could. On each occasion ... except the last ... they had been together, but since that visit of Manny's had been to buy material for her father, she now nostalgically counted it as Dad's as well.

Yes, Dad's, she thought lovingly, yet Justin's, too, for Justin Welsh had turned up unexpectedly, making that shopping chore more a pleasure than a daughterly duty. Making it much more, as things had turned out, for Justin had asked her to marry him, and she had said she would. Now, after more than four weeks they had agreed upon, she was back to keep her word.

She was in the foyer by now and stepping out bravely. The hotel did not know about Justin yet, only about Father's sudden death, and Manny knew what the receptionist would say, and tried to brace herself.

She was right.

'Welcome, Miss Norbert,' the clerk said tactfully. 'We're happy to have you again. We're only sorry...'

'Yes. Thank you,' Manny murmured, and bit on her lip.

'We've reserved your old room, we knew you'd like that. One night only, your letter said?'

'Yes. You see, I ... well, as a matter of fact I ...' But Manny did not go on, for two more guests had come into the lobby. As she followed the bellboy to the lift she was suddenly aware that she would not have told the receptionist anyway, even though women like to hear about weddings, even though brides-to-be like, or are said to like, to tell. But, though not understanding why, she knew she would not tell.

She talked weather-talk to the boy until they reached her floor and he carried her bag to Seventy-five and opened the door. She gave him a coin, waited for him to leave, then crossed at once to the window. She was here at last, here to fulfil a promise, so now perhaps she would lose some of her nagging unrest. She looked hopefully down.

Sydney was the same city, she found, only more so, for big cities behaved like that, leave them a day and they grew a year. Yet some things did not grow, the park across the street for instance, the fountain in the park ... the small stone church tucked between two towering office blocks. The church where to-morrow she and Justin would be married.

Now Manny stood very still ... and very anxiously, had she only realised ... waiting for the previous magic to grab her again, for the romance, the enchantment, the thrall of being in love to begin a second time. She waited, but it did not come, only a flatness, almost a deadness remained. It was because Dad was dead, she told herself sensitively, it was because in this familiar hotel she was suffering her recent bereavement afresh. When Justin met her tonight it would be different, she could turn a page as pages must be turned, she could start the next chapter in her life.

She crossed back to where the boy had placed her bag and began unpacking. First of all she took out the dress. It was blue because Justin had ordered blue after he had proposed to her, and after she, bewildered in the beginning, then running with a sweet wild wind, had said Yes.

'Blue for true love, Manny,' Justin had stipulated, 'because that's what I have for you, my sweet, I have true love.'

'Yes, Justin.' Actually Manny had said it a little uncertainly, she now remembered, uncertain that all this was really happening to her. For though she had liked Justin Welsh the moment she had met him when he had joined the sand-mining company up at Soleil Bay it had not been *that* kind of liking, or so she had thought at the time. No, it had been more the attraction of one young contemporary to another, especially when the other was a tall, fair, extremely good-looking man with a smooth, winning way. Also, and Manny had to admit it, Dad's maddening unenthusiasm had teased it along further. Also it had been *him*—Huw Grant, the new Soleil Bay boss. Right from his arrival at Soleil, mainly for his marked victimisation of Justin, Manny had perversely turned to Justin and loathed Grant.

Yet in spite of the fact that Grant had come to direct the sand-mining, a project that distressed her artist father very much, Dad, surprisingly, had taken to the fellow.

'The workers were getting slapdash under old Peter,' he had said. Peter was the retiring boss. 'They needed a younger, tougher man. Also a man with a dream left in him. This Huw Grant has that.'

'You're only flattered because he's bought a picture,' Manny, unimpressed, had returned.

'Three, Emmanuelle. Also ordered a mural for his firm's Sydney headquarters. Also asked for my advice for restoration after the rutile has been won. What's got into you, Manny? You seem to have a down on the man already.'

Manny could have told him, but she knew it would have sounded petty. To have answered that she did not like Grant because the men, all her friends, so far did not warm to him would have seemed trivial, and then to tell Dad that an actual near-hate had arisen because of his picking on Justin would have been a mistake.

For her father did not care for Justin at all.

'Why don't you like him, Dad?' Manny had asked on several occasions. 'You must have a reason.'

'He's just not right, Manny. Besides, when I was talking with Huw Grant——'

'*Him.*'

'Yes, him.' Her father had looked stern.

'The gang,' Manny had passed on maliciously, 're-gret the day Grant came.'

'At this moment they do, but wait for a few weeks when their conditions change for the better. Peter was lenient enough, but not interested any more. The place was falling back. This man is different.'

'Another picture order on the way, Mr Norbert?'

'I wish it was a different daughter, my present one is a disaster. For heaven's sake, Manny, give Grant time!'

'Will he give it to Justin?'

'Oh, yes, I heard there was trouble there.'

'Trouble!' scoffed Manny. 'He never lets up on Justin. Actually it's only a silly matter of the books not being quite correct, Justin tells me, and everyone knows that that can happen in any corporation, that in the end it all comes out right.'

'It is not a silly matter, it shouldn't happen, and it can't come out right.'

'You're biased, Father.'

'I am not, I am entirely with Huw in this, and I don't blame him for giving Welsh his marching orders. Why, even old Peter saw through the fellow.'

But Manny had not been listening to the previous boss's attitude to Justin, only to *this* boss's.

'Marching orders!' she had disbelieved. 'You can't mean——'

'Dismissal? The boot? I do. And why not?'

'Why not!' Manny had all but exploded. This was now, not the Dark Ages, men could not be tossed out for a small mistake, it just couldn't happen.

But it had happened.

One day Justin had been working on the project, the next day he was gone. Manny had been incensed, and so had the men, especially Larry, the shop steward as well as the oldest and most vocal hand.

'I reckon I've never seen anyone go so fast,' he had disapproved to Manny. 'One minute Welsh is among us, the next minute he's history. The boys don't like it. Not that they particularly liked Welsh, but——'

But Manny, who did like Welsh, liked it even less.

'It's not fair, Dad,' she had said angrily later.

'Forget it, Manny, and go down to Sydney and get me some material for this company mural order. I'll need ...'

Glad to get away from such a man as Huw Grant, Manny had gone, almost 'forgetting' as she had been directed by her father, for after all, her association with Justin had been very brief, quite light, rather unimportant ... or so she had thought until she had met him again on her assignment for Dad, met him outside this hotel.

'Justin!' she had exclaimed in complete surprise.

'Manny.' There had been no surprise from him, only a very apparent—and very flattering—satisfaction.

'What a chance meeting,' she had murmured, femininely pleased with his pleasure in her.

'Except that it isn't,' he had smiled significantly, 'except that I've been planning this from the day I was kicked out.'

'Were you really kicked out, Justin? I never learned for sure whether you were dismissed or whether you resigned.'

'Much as I would readily have resigned from Grant's authority I would never have resigned from any place where *you* were, Manny.'

Manny remembered saying a little hurriedly: 'So Huw Grant actually——'

'Yes, Huw Grant, actually.' A lopsided grin.

'Larry and the boys were up in arms,' Manny had reported. She had not added that the storm had been rather shortlived and that everything seemed fairly amiable again, if a little cool on Larry's part, but then Larry was the men's representative, very dedicated, inclined to be fiery, and instinctively wary of bosses.

'Yes,' Justin had nodded, 'and I appreciate that, but I don't want to talk shop, a closed shop as it's become for me, thanks to Grant. No, I want to talk about—us.'

'Us?' she queried.

'You, me. But where, Manny? In your hotel coffee shop?'

'Is the talk private?' Manny had asked that because the hotel coffee shop was not.

'Very. On the other hand, I want to tell the world.'

'Tell the world what, Justin?'

'Tell them I'm in love with the loveliest of girls and that she's in love with me.'

'But, Justin, I'm not!'

'Not the loveliest?'

'Not that either, but I meant not in love with——'

'Aren't you? Aren't you, Manny?' Justin had come a step closer, and, bemused, Manny had let him take her arm and lead her over to the park.

There on a bench he had wasted no time.

'This is no chance meeting, Manny,' he had repeated. 'Before I was kicked out I happened to be in the office on the day Grant commissioned that mural from your father and your father accepted it, adding that he would send you down to Sydney for the material he would require. I heard Grant ask him where you would stay.'

'The nerve of him!' she exclaimed.

'The stuffiness, you mean. He was probably making sure it was a respectable inn and not some dive that the corporation might not approve.'

'But I'm nothing to do with the company.'

'No, but with a fat commission like a mural would be then your father is. No doubt Grant was afraid of another blot on the copybook.'

'Another?'

'Mine,' Justin had reminded her with a shrug. 'According to Grant I made many blots. But evidently your father's choice of hostelries satisfied His Nibs. Grant accepted it, anyway, and I' ... a grin ... 'duly took note.'

'Yes, Justin?' Again Manny recalled asking.

'I took note because I knew I would be coming here to meet you. Yes, darling' ... darling? ... 'even then I knew that. Don't ask me how, Manny, I just knew. I love you, darling, and we're going to be married. It's as simple and wonderful as that.'

Manny had stared at Justin in disbelief, but it had been an exciting, quite thrilling incredulity. Justin could be right, she had thought a little deliriously, all the time I believed we were only friends up at Soleil we really could have been—something else.

After all, I'm a very inexperienced person when it comes to love, there's never been much love opportunity at the Bay for me to find out. But—*marriage*?

She must have said it aloud, for Justin immediately had rushed in ... rushed very eloquently.

'It has to be marriage, Manny. Marriage the estimable estate, the natural conclusion, the logical end of the lane. Also' ... and a sneer now ... 'a blow to King Grant.'

'What do you mean?'

'The fellow's attracted to you, surely you have seen that.'

'He dislikes me as intensely as I dislike him,' Manny assured him.

'Love and hate are very akin.'

'Not on my part, nor, I'm sure, on his.'

'Don't be so sure. As a fellow male I can tell you ... But why should I tell you anything but *my* feelings for you?' Justin's well-manicured hand had touched the silk above Manny's accelerating heart.

'Feelings that have suddenly sprung up just to spite King Grant?' Manny had said it shrewdly and been rather surprised at herself, for she was not naturally a very shrewd person. At once she had felt ashamed, too, for Justin had looked disappointed in her.

'Oh, Manny!' he had reproached.

He had taken her hand but said nothing, just held it, and then it all had started, slowly at first, then faster, then a veritable whirlwind. The music of a city had played for Manny, the fountain in the park had played for her, and she had fallen in love with love and the man who had given her the idea.

'Oh, Justin,' she had said.

'I knew it, *I knew it*. When, Manny?'

'When?'

'Marriage the estimable estate, the natural conclusion, the end of the lane.'

'There was also something else you said,' she had reminded him. 'A blow to King Grant.'

'Forget that. Forget everything. Only think of us. When? Tomorrow? It can be done with a special licence.'

'No, Justin, I would want to talk with Dad first.'

'But you're twenty-one.'

'He's still my father.'

'And he doesn't approve of me. Oh, yes, I know that. Undoubtedly Grant has had a few words to say.'

'Father wouldn't listen to false words.'

'False words can be put very convincingly.'

'He still wouldn't listen, Justin, but he'll listen to me, he always does.'

'And you'll listen to him, listen to him tell you No. But I love you, Manny. If you loved me you would agree now.'

'I do love you.' Manny *had* in that racing moment. 'But, Justin, it still can't be now. Please be understanding when I tell you that Dad has to be told.'

For a few moments, she recalled, Justin had sat silent. Then he had smiled.

'He'll promptly tell Grant all about it,' he had anticipated. 'Your father and the king have become very buddy-buddy. Grant's bubble of pride will have a pin put in it. All right then, dutiful daughter, I'll regretfully wait. Go back with our message of love, our intention to do something about it, then return here and——' Justin had dropped her hand to take her in his arms instead, then to kiss her.

'One month, no more,' he had said when they had drawn apart again. He had taken a piece of paper from his pocket and written on it. When he had passed it to Manny she had read:

'Wednesday, 18th: Meet my beloved.

'Thursday, 19th: Marry her.'

'Justin, you're the maddest thing!' she had half laughed, half cried at the same time.

'Yet the dearest?'

'The dearest.' Of course he was the dearest, who else would have written such a mad, dear note? If somewhere in Manny a voice had suggested that perhaps Justin was only the dearest because there was no one else to be dear, she had not listened.

She had heard him assure her that he would make all the arrangements ... that *that*, pointing romantically, would be their church ... that she had only to turn up on the appointed day.

She had been whirling with that sweet wind by then, dancing to the wind's music. 'Of course I'll turn up,' she had said.

She had not. Not at the arranged time, but Justin would understand that. Her father, though living in obscure Soleil Bay, was not an obscure person, and the death of the noted artist had been written up in all the papers. Justin would know she could not come then but that she would come as soon as she could.

That soon as she could had been today, two weeks

after their rendezvous, but Manny had written a short letter to an address Justin had said would find him. She had told him she would be at the Hotel Southerly again ... or in front of their church ... that he could contact her at either place. Perhaps he had been here already and left a message.

She did not go down to find out, though; suddenly her feet seemed leaden. She wished, as she had wished ever since her father suddenly had left her, that she had had time to tell Dad, get him to understand. But she had not had time. She had barely returned to the Bay with his material than he had collapsed, then died. After that everything had gone by in a daze. Only the comfort of Justin's declared love had seen her through, or so she had believed. As soon as everything was over she had made her plans.

She had not told anyone at the Works, she had no reason to, she was not employed there. She had simply lived with Dad in a beach cottage adjoining the sand-mining project that had come along to upset the tranquillity of their piece of coast, and what she did was her own concern.

She had not spoken to Huw Grant at all.

She had gone quietly away one morning, *this* morning sorry she had not found time to say goodbye to Larry, some of her other friends, but now at last she was here. Here to marry Justin. Here to turn a page. Begin again. Suddenly restless, Manny paced the room ... went to the window once more ... came back and sat on the bed. She wished Justin would come.

She took some things out of her bag, put the blue

dress under a concealing cover. Otherwise, she thought, the maid might come in to turn down the bed and see it, and she did not want that. After all, the hotel only associated her with Father, not with——

When she looked through the window the next time it was growing dark, the room that had been afternoon-gold when the bellboy had opened the door now had violet shadows. Manny flicked on a light and willed the telephone to ring.

She poured herself a glass of water. She would have preferred coffee, and she could have called for it, but she was still leaden.

Why didn't the telephone ring?

She could still see the church clearly. It had a few sprinkles of sunlight left. When the sun went entirely she would go, too, she would go down to the church. Possibly Justin was too shy to come up here ... Justin shy? ... but he would go there, she was quite sure he would.

But if Manny was sure of Justin, slowly, insidiously yet progressively with each progressing minute, she became sharply aware that she was beginning to feel less sure of herself. She tried to stifle the unsureness, to disregard it, but it was no use, it still persisted.

What, she thought in accelerating panic, do I really know about Justin except smiling blue eyes, an apt way of talking and a smooth way with love? What, for that matter, is love? Justin had described it poetically as the laneway to marriage, he had said that marriage itself was the end of the lane, the

natural conclusion. But he also had included their
own marriage as a score against Huw Grant. A pin in
Grant's pride bubble, he had said. A blow to King
Grant. Manny felt herself flinch distastefully at that.

Accepting that Justin loved her, which she supposed she must, how much did she love him back?
Not like a lot, enjoy a great deal, but *love*? If she
had not run into him again after he had left Soleil
Bay would she have forgotten him? She had been
taken by surprise, a lovely surprise that would have
turned the head of any girl, but without that encounter would she have remembered him? Would
she have—loved?

No, Manny suddenly knew, I would not, and I
can't. Also I can't marry Justin.

To be quite fair, quite certain, she crossed to the
window again and looked at the church, looked for
reassurance for herself and Justin. There was none.
She gazed at the spire pointing its finger to heaven
and knew with certainty that it was not to be *their*
heaven. There was a drumming in her head, a spin-
ning, there was a giddiness, but in the middle of the
small nightmare there was a core of positiveness there
was no denying.

It had all been fun, even a little magic. She was
sorry for Justin, sorry for herself, sorry over the whole
situation, but whichever way she looked at it, it
still meant nothing. She knew she would have forgotten Justin, that she would forget him now. She
had already.

She turned away from the window and came back
to the room and took up a jacket. She was going

down to the church to see if Justin was there. If he was not, she had his address and she would find him, tell him. It would be hard, they would both hate it, but ... but ...

For the first time for weeks, and Manny realised it now, she felt a lightness and a vast relief.

Down in the lobby she did not check for any message, she simply made her way as fast as she could across the street. She only stopped when she reached the church.

'Good evening, Miss Norbert.' The voice cut into her new realisation, a realisation she had not had time to evaluate yet, only embrace. It was not Justin's voice, it was too clipped, too clear, Justin rather drawled his words, almost tasted them. Also he had never called her Miss Norbert even at their first meeting.

Manny whirled round and met the cool gleam of silver eyes. Not blue but silver. There was only one person she knew with silver eyes, he was Huw Grant.

'Good evening,' Manny responded automatically. Then, unable to stop herself, she demanded angrily: 'Why are you here?'

'Certainly not to be married,' he replied, 'even though it's the accepted function of a church. But then' ... still clear and clipped ... 'you're not going to be married either, are you? Not, anyway, to Welsh. Not today.'

'It was tomorrow.' Manny heard her own voice correcting him, but she was not conscious of mouthing the words herself.

'Nor tomorrow either,' he tacked on.

Not waiting this time for any response Huw Grant crossed to her side, took hold of her arm, then impelled her across to the park.

CHAPTER TWO

MANNY'S first impulse was to push Huw Grant away, but people were passing, so with difficulty she refrained. She was also obliged to refrain by the pressure of his hand.

'Control yourself,' Huw Grant said.

'Step away from me and I'll try,' she replied.

Huw Grant did.

Presently he said in a less clipped voice: 'I'm sorry I broke it like that.'

'Broke?' she queried.

'Broke the news about you not marrying Welsh,' he told her.

... A conclusion I reached on my own accord ten minutes ago, Manny thought, but she was not going to let *him* know. Instead she asked coldly: 'Why would you think I was interested in marriage?'

'According to Welsh it was more than just an interest, it was a fait accompli.'

'You've seen Justin?'

'Welsh? Yes.'

'And he told you this?'

'Yes.'

'Told you that he wouldn't be here to——'

'To marry you? Yes.'

Manny put aside an indignation against Justin who at least could have told her first and instead focused on Grant. 'Were you surprised?' she enquired coldly.

'Oh, no, not with him.'

'You really mean what you've built him into,' she accused.

'No, I mean what he *is*.'

'Oh, that again!'

'By that remark I take it you're referring to what happened up at Soleil?' Huw Grant asked calmly.

'Yes. Your victimisation of Justin.'

'Will you listen to the truth?'

'No, it would all be lies.'

He gave a small sigh. 'All right then, we'll leave it there.' He waited a moment, then began again. 'As you know, I discharged Welsh, and I would have finished it at that had you not interfered.'

'I?' she queried.

'You wrote to Welsh.'

'Yes ... yes, I did, but how would you know?'

'You foolishly forgot that the cottage mail for convenience' sake goes with the company correspondence.'

'But you couldn't ... you didn't ...'

'See and then open your letter? Yes.'

'You ... why, you ...' Manny spluttered furiously.

'It was one of the last things your father asked of me,' he told her blandly.

'To open my letters?'

'To watch you and Welsh. From your letter to Welsh I found out that you were going down to meet him, I read for what reason, so I came south as well. I went to the address you had on your envelope, and thrashed the thing out.'

'What do you mean by "thing"?' she demanded.

'This thing, Miss Norbert, that is not going to take place.' He nodded to the church. 'Your marriage.'

'You must be mad!'

'No, only resolved not to let it happen again.'

'Again?' Manny queried.

But Huw Grant did not answer that. For a moment he stood very still, his face enigmatical, then he gave a little shake of himself and changed the trend.

'Have you eaten yet?' he asked.

'No.'

'Then we'll do so together.'

'I'm not hungry.'

'Nonetheless you will eat.' Again he took hold of her. Before Manny could stage another protest he had hailed a taxi and put her in. He gave the driver an address.

They sat silently in the cab, Manny longing to snatch a look at the tall, dark, silver-eyed man beside her, but steeling herself. What, she wondered, was this all about? If Huw Grant had prevailed upon Justin not to keep his promise how had he achieved it? Undoubtedly that wretched accounts affair that Grant had built up to dismissal proportions had been his trump card, but even so would Justin have let it interfere with his personal life? ... *with his impending marriage*?

She did not ask this, however, until they had reached the restaurant of his choice, and he had seated her at the table the waiter had allotted.

'Assuming you were right about Justin, I mean about his——' she began.

'Discrepancy? I was right.'

She ignored this interruption and started again.

'Assuming you were right, then how could it prevent ... how could it cancel ...'

'Tomorrow's ceremony? My dear child, how can you marry someone who won't be there?'

She had stiffened at his patronage, but what came after it loosened her barely controlled rage.

'How do you know he won't be there? You can't actually stop him.'

'I have actually stopped him ... with the help of the law.'

'What?'

'The law, I said.'

'You mean—you really mean you——'

'Yes.' The answer was quite indifferent, indifferent to her feelings, supremely indifferent, she knew now, to any feelings of Justin's.

'You reported him for a trivial thing like that?' she seethed.

'It all depends on your definition of trivia. I'm afraid mine differs from yours.'

'So for that you gave him into custody?'

'No, but I threatened to do so if he didn't tell me everything he had in mind regarding you, then when he did tell me I threatened him again should he try to carry it out.'

'Carry out marrying me?'

'Yes.'

'And Justin agreed?'

A thin smile, then again: 'Yes. Of course he had to agree,' Grant added at once. 'He could scarcely marry you, could he, if he was put away.'

'Put away?' she echoed.

'I think you follow me.'

'I do, and you're incredible!'

'The situation is incredible, Miss Norbert. I never dreamed that Welsh would turn up a second time.'

'You knew him before?'

'I did.'

'And it prejudiced you?'

'Prejudiced?' He echoed that, then gave a tight laugh. 'That's a very pale word.'

Manny was not listening. 'You never gave him a chance,' she said hotly. 'Right from the beginning, Justin's beginning, your mind was closed.' She stopped rather abruptly, for her glance had fallen to the man's hands, and she noticed how strongly they were clasped, so strongly that the knucklebones protruded hard and white.

'He,' she heard him say sharply, 'gave nobody a chance.'

A few minutes went by with neither of them speaking.

'At least,' Manny defended, 'Justin didn't embarrass me. At least I was allowed to know.' (Know something I already knew for myself, she could have added, but she kept it jealously to herself.)

'I think you really mean he didn't leave you waiting at the church, like in the song.'

'You're hateful!' Manny pushed aside her plate. 'Do I have to eat all this?'

'You can leave it ... make up for it tomorrow.'

Manny said bitterly: 'Wherever I am tomorrow.'

'You'll be with me, returning to Soleil Bay.'

'Oh, no, I won't,' she assured him.

'You have plenty of money, then?' he asked almost idly.

'I have sufficient.'

'Sufficient for how long?' Huw Grant paused. 'Sufficient for how much?'

'What do you mean "For how much?"'

'I mean for how much repayment, Miss Norbert? I hate to bring this up so soon, but my firm had paid an advance to your father for the work he was commissioned to do, and it was a very substantial advance. It was——' He quoted a figure.

Manny sat like a stone. Dad had never told her ... she had never dreamed ...

'I'm sorry.' He said that a second time, but for several more minutes Manny still sat rigid.

'But how could I help?' At last she found words. 'How could I ever cancel such a debt?'

He looked at her levelly, the silver eyes compelling her. 'You could,' he said quietly, 'complete the work yourself.'

'I? But I only dabble.'

'Yes, I know you only dabble, and I've criticised your father frequently about that. I told him that if he hadn't been so good you might have been good, that you were finding your artistic outlet in his art, never your own.'

'How did you know about my art or lack of art?' she asked.

'He showed me some of your work. He was very

proud of it. Had he lived he had intended to enlist your help in the mural he *had already been paid for*.'

The terrifying fact that the work had been paid for temporarily missed Manny. Instead she protested emphatically: 'I could never take over where Dad left off, and I could never have helped Dad in a big thing like that.'

'You could.' A pause. 'You can.'

'But——'

'Oh, not immediately, perhaps. You could find your feet, at least your fingers, at first. Do a few tentative sketches, even keep the pot boiling by a picture or two. I'm sure you would find a buyer.' He gave an encouraging smile to which Manny did not respond.

'To boil a pot you require a kitchen,' she said hollowly.

'I follow you,' he nodded. 'You're saying you wouldn't have that.'

'Yes, I am. I don't even have a house—we only rented the cottage. Artists don't make much money, Mr Grant. This money would have been Dad's first large fee, in spite of his big name.'

'Now a fee you must pay back,' he reminded her ruthlessly.

'I can't pay it back! Why, the material alone cost the earth. I should know, I bought it.'

'And bought yourself a deal of trouble on the same city visit,' he said drily. 'Well, if no mural is forthcoming the money has to be returned. It's as basic as that.'

'I haven't got the money,' Manny said again. 'Why are you so insistent? Has Justin's affair upset your accounting so much that you're not giving me time even to try to return the material?' Secretly she said it without hope, for her father had already started on the canvas, opened every pot and jar—he had always done that.

'No,' Huw Grant answered, 'I'm insistent because I want you to *try*. I've seen your work, and you're good.'

'I'm not good,' she contradicted.

'No, perhaps that was the wrong word, I should have said promising. You are not' ... a slight smile that lifted the rather deep lines in a face not ready, Manny unwillingly conceded, for such lines yet ... 'quite fitted to the adjective "good". However, we'll leave that and get back to what I propose. I propose to take you home tomorrow to Soleil Bay, set you up in the cottage again. After all, why not, your father told me his lease still had some months to run, and can you afford to forfeit that?'

'But it was a weekly lease.'

'It might have been once, but when I gave the order to Mr Norbert ... *and the advance* ... he promptly altered that. I suppose he didn't want to be concerned over offputting things like rents when he had a brush in his hand.'

'Dad never told me.'

'... But you never told him, did you?' He looked at her meaningly.

'How could I—if you're referring to Justin?'

'I was.'

'Then how could I when Dad was already distrusting Justin?'

'Yes, he would distrust him, I think.'

'Distrust him because of you.' Manny looked directly at Huw Grant, but he merely shrugged.

'There's one more thing I want to say,' he told Manny.

'Yes?'

'I've seen your father's theme for this mural. It's —well, it's quite wonderful.'

'I know. I've seen it, too. And you would still ask me——'

'No, I would expect you. I would expect you to do your father proud. You loved him, didn't you?'

'Yes.'

'Then?'

Manny bit her lip, bit deeply. 'I'd like to, I suppose, but I couldn't.'

'You could try. And the only place to do it would be up there at Soleil where the theme is set. It would have to be there. Miss Norbert, can you refuse?'

'I can refuse you,' she assured him.

'But your father's trust? The place you love? For you do love it, don't you? I've noticed your absorption in it often.'

Had he? Manny had never noticed. Aloud she said unwillingly: 'I was there from a child.'

'Which is not so far away now,' he suggested with another smile.

'I'm twenty-one.'

'Of course. You were being married.' He waited a watchful moment, then tossed: 'Will we have coffee, or does it keep you awake?'

'It doesn't matter, I have all day tomorrow, all the rest of the days.'

'Not on my schedule. I always leave early, I intend to be out of Sydney and on the highway by eight.'

'Yes, one travels fast ... alone.'

'I don't intend to be alone. Listen to me, Manny, or do you prefer Emmanuelle? It's rather a big name for a small person.'

'It was my grandmother's name, and Miss Norbert will do.'

'Listen to me, Manny, you can't afford to turn this offer down, and you know it.'

'But I can't do as you suggest for another reason. I can't possibly go back, not now, not now that I've left. I—I would be embarrassed.'

'You mean because you would be returning *un*married?'

'Yes.'

'But who else besides the principals knew, you young idiot?'

'No one, or so I thought, but now I know you.'

'And that would embarrass you?'

She half turned away.

He waited a moment, then said: 'Come back, Manny, come back to love, for that's your father's theme, you know that. If you don't, what else is there for you? City jobs are at a premium unless you're specifically qualified for something.'

'And I'm not,' she admitted ruefully.

'Then how, with city rents, city prices, can you hope to pay back your father's advance?'

'Always money,' Manny quivered.

'I'm open to an alternative.' He said it quietly. He was looking hard at her again, but this time his silver eyes were narrowed.

'Like what?' she muttered.

'Like—love, but personal love, not love on a canvas.' He said it lightly, almost in banter.

'I've had enough of love,' she answered stonily.

'Oh, no, you haven't, and that's your trouble, you've never even begun.'

She looked at him quickly, wondering how he could know, how he could have read her. She looked sensitively away again.

But at once she became sharply aware that Huw Grant was still staring at her, unashamedly probing her. She heard him ask: Well?'

'Thank you,' she answered, 'I will have coffee.'

'You know I wasn't asking that.'

'Then I suppose thank you to the other, too, Mr Grant. What else is there?'

'I think you should call me Huw.'

'Grant will do.'

'It will not do—not, anyway, after we pick up Jane.'

'Pick up Jane?' Manny picked up herself.

'That explanation can wait until we do pick her up,' he dismissed. 'Immediately we'll skip that coffee after all, get you back to the hotel for a good night's sleep and an early take-off.' Once more he managed the situation.

In the taxi he told her he had booked into another inn.

'I didn't want to intrude,' he said.

'Thank you,' she said coldly.

'You must try to relax,' he said at the hotel door, the door at which Manny had paused earlier, then taken a deep steadying breath to help her to walk in.

'Yes.'

'Then goodnight, Manny. You've had a busy day.' He stepped back from her, then stepped away.

Up in her room Manny undressed quickly, slipped into bed without any of her usual preliminaries.

Today she had come down to Sydney to join Justin. She had not joined him. Tomorrow she had had a tryst with Justin to marry him. She was not going to keep it. Sleep, that man, that Huw Grant, had said, you've had a busy day; relax. A sob started in her throat, but by some odd quirk it did not mature. Instead a weary little grunt emerged, and, not knowing when, or how she could, Manny slept.

CHAPTER THREE

'You obeyed me, I see.' These were Huw Grant's first words when Manny met him the next morning.

He had not waited in the hotel lobby as she had expected, but, having asked for her room number, had come right to her door. The moment she answered the knock and opened up he walked in.

That was aggravating enough, but his 'obeyed' was further fuel.

'What do you mean by "obeyed"?' Manny demanded touchily.

'You did as I ordered, you slept, you relaxed, I can see it by your eyes. What colour are they? You're an artist, are they gold, fawn or brown?'

'Pickle.' She was still irritated. 'Did you have to come right up?'

'Yes, to help you with your luggage.'

'The bellboy——'

'Has only one pair of hands, rather small hands, and brides bring along the earth.'

'But I'm not a bride, remember.'

'No, I saw to that.'

You didn't, though, Manny retorted inwardly, I did it myself. Outwardly she asked: 'Did you have breakfast?'

'No, I'll have it with you on the road.' He was gazing in disbelief at her single piece of luggage. 'Is there really only one bag?'

'One bag.'

'What's that?' He pointed to the blue gown still hanging in the wardrobe, covered with a dust protector but a frilled hem still showing.

'It's a dress.'

'I can see that, but—a special dress?'

'Why should it be special?'

'Hung with such loving care? Blue?' He had crossed to the closet to finger it and he looked back at Manny. 'Blue for true love?' he probed.

For a treacherous moment Manny felt the tears pricking, not for Justin, she knew that now, but for something that had finished before it even started.

'Manny,' said Huw Grant, and he came back to her. In a sudden gentle voice he asked her: 'Was it to be the dress?'

'Yes.'

'Then we must fold it carefully.'

'We'll do nothing of the sort. I'm not taking it.'

'Not taking it?' he echoed.

'I don't want it, not ever. I'm leaving it behind.'

'You are not.'

'It's my dress, I can do what I like with it.'

'Except leave it here. Good grief, woman, how can you be so daft? The hotel would only contact you about it, a dress like that, and a blue dress to boot, wouldn't fool even a dumb male, let alone a practised chambermaid. It fairly screams bride, can't you see that?'

'Brides wear white,' she corrected.

'Sometimes they wear blue.'

'For true love,' Manny finished for him.

'I see you understand me. Pack it up then and we'll get going.'

'I'm not taking it,' she repeated stubbornly.

'Why?'

'Because I'll never wear it.'

'I can follow that, but you still can't leave it swaying here for the maid to find and the clerk to send on, the whole damn business to start all over again.'

'It won't.'

'I don't believe you, in which case if you won't fold it, I will.' He started to struggle with folds and frills.

'That's not the way,' she began.

'Then I'll carry it as it is,' he exploded, and he took her bag in one hand and swung the dress with the other.

'It will dangle in the dust.'

'But you no longer care,' he reminded her. 'However' ... hitching it up a few inches ... 'I won't soil it. Jane at least will be interested.'

'Jane?' she queried.

'She's the pick-up I mentioned yesterday. Well, come on.'

'I have to settle my account,' she pointed out.

'It's settled.'

She looked at him with dislike. 'No doubt to be taken out of any money I earn later.'

'Money you earn? You'll be cancelling a debt, not gathering shekels.' He walked out of the room as he said it, then strode down the corridor to the lift. Manny had to hurry to catch up to him.

Down in the lobby the receptionist started to come out to see Manny off, but the sight of Huw Grant marching determinedly in front of Miss Norbert with an elegant blue gown over his arm stopped her.

Wretchedly Manny mumbled: 'Goodbye, Miss Clarke, thank you.' She caught Grant up in the street.

He was walking along quite unconcerned by the amused glances he was collecting because of the dress. He was larger than Manny had thought, and even taller than Justin. It was the girth of him, a solidity that the slimmer Justin did not have, that made him appear more substance than height, she thought.

'You're big,' she said on an impulse.

'It runs in the family, you'll see that when you meet Jane.'

'Your daughter?'

'I'm not married. Anyway, do I look old enough to have a fifteen-year-old child?'

'You do at times.'

'Times like chasing trouble as I am now? No, Jane is my niece. Here's the waggon.'

Manny had noticed his estate waggon up at Soleil Bay but only parked in its garage; he always seemed to be driving the sand buggy. She stood while he put in the bag, put in the dress, then opened the door beside the driver and nodded her in.

'Perhaps your niece would like this seat,' Manny demurred.

'Jane will sit at the back,' he assured her.

'There's room in the front, too.'

'You'll have to sit in the middle, then, because I can tell you I won't have Jane beside me with her baubles and bows.'

'I could sit at the back.' Manny did not want to sit close to him.

'Just get in,' he ordered, and gave her a push. He got in himself and they started off.

He did not speak as he threaded a way through the city snarl of traffic, but once away from the crush he had time for other things.

'We'll breakfast by the Hawkesbury, it's a lovely river.'

'But Jane——'

'Will breakfast, as usual, at her school.'

'She's at boarding school?'

'Yes, but leaving today. Her father has been directed to a temporary post in the States, and Glenys, my older sister, is taking the opportunity to accompany her husband. This is Glen's first overseas binge, and I want it to be a good one. So I'm taking Jane over.' He heaved a sigh as he said it, and Manny suspected it was not really as generous-hearted of him as his words tried to convey.

'Couldn't the school have done that?' she suggested.

'Not during vacation, which it happens to be right now.'

'Some schools accept vacation boarders.'

'Some, but not Jane's school, or' ... a grimace ... 'it could be not Jane.'

'You said your older sister. Is there another?'

'Yes.'

'Couldn't she——' Manny began.

'No!' His voice came quite sharp. 'No, she could not.'

There was silence again.

They had bacon and eggs at a river house overlooking a sweep of wooded inlets and mangrove mazes. The water through the leaves of the trees was emerald silk and the half fresh, half salt tang of it gave a zest to the hot breads that came later with the tall jugs of steaming coffee.

At first Manny tried to be aloof, but when Huw Grant began talking about Soleil Bay, she had to give in.

'Yes,' she admitted, 'it's my place.'

'Yet you would have left it?'

'"Whither thou goest, I will go",' she quoted deliberately.

'Why, thank you, Manny,' Huw Grant accepted falsely.

'You know I wasn't referring to you, that I meant——'

'Yes, I know that a woman must follow her man.'

His authoritative male acceptance of her quotation, even though she first had introduced it, irritated Manny. In her exasperation she lied: 'And I shall follow Justin one day.'

He looked at her with narrowed eyes. 'Not if I'm around.'

'What did you say?'

'I told you not if I'm around.'

'I may not be around myself,' she pointed out.

'Then I'll still be there, because I shall have followed you.'

She stared at him. 'What on earth for?'

'I could say for love,' he baited her, 'but I won't, I'll tell the truth. It would be to check on Welsh.'

'You're really obsessed with Justin, aren't you?' she jeered.

He did not answer that, he poured more coffee, and once again Manny saw his whitened knucklebones on his tightened hands, sensed his barely contained anger.

'The gang didn't like your treatment of Justin,' she dared.

'They're over it now,' he shrugged.

'Larry——'

'Larry will come round in the end. His sort take

longer, that's all. There's always a Larry in every outfit.'

'I think,' said Manny in sudden inspiration, 'that once Justin was a Larry in one of your past projects and that he did *not* come round, whereupon your injured pride never forgave him. I think that's why you won't accept him now.'

He looked at her pityingly for a very long moment, and Manny squirmed. But:

'Keep thinking,' was all he scornfully advised. Presently he said: 'If you're finished we'll get going. I rang Jane's place of learning, or so her parents are hoping, and said I'd collect her by eleven.'

They went back to the waggon.

They followed the highway to Newcastle, then turned west into the vineyard country where Jane's school was situated. It was beautiful terrain, shallow rolling hills all under purple grape.

'It's too good for little St Trinians,' Huw Grant grunted of the passing scene, 'all those young horrors want are hockey fields and Coke.'

'Does Jane?'

'Jane?' He slackened speed slightly. 'No, not Jane.' He gave Manny a sudden appealing glance. 'I want your help with her.'

'How?'

'She's a handful, or would be if she could get away with it.'

'I think you mean not just hockey and Coke,' observed Manny.

'I mean that precisely. She's as precocious a fifteen as you'll ever meet. She shouldn't be coming with us really, not to male-dominated Soleil Bay, but——'

'But?'

'Well, to tell you the awful truth, though I couldn't tell her parents, the school doesn't want her any more.'

'She was expelled?'

'No, nothing like that. It was merely suggested by the head when I telephoned Miss Fitzroy that if another school could be found for Jane they wouldn't be unduly upset.'

'I see, so what do you want me to do?'

'Watch her.'

'Oh, no, Mr Grant!' she protested.

'Well, get her confidence at least. Be mates with her. After all, you're round the same age.'

'Fifteen and twenty-one? A girl and a woman?'

'Are you that? Oh, yes, I know you're a marriage-able female, but—a woman?' Again he took his eyes off the wheel for a moment and his glance was quizzical. 'I haven't noticed any womanhood myself, but then, of course, I wasn't Justin Welsh. We turn here.' He took a side lane, wound with it for some distance, reached a low red building with the customary school wings surrounding a quadrangle, then pulled up.

'St Helen's, not St Trinians,' Manny remarked, looking at the name on the gate.

'I won't be long,' he replied.

He was only minutes. He returned looking thunderous, followed by a tall young girl. Manny had a quick impression of early physical maturity as well as graceful height in Grant's charge, but it was only fleeting, for her attention was on the girl's marked prettiness—outstanding in spite of a quite appalling make-up.

Grant's first words as he threw in the girl's bags were: 'Wipe that stuff off your face, you young madam.'

'Uncle Huw——'

'And take off those jangles.' Presumably he meant the dripping ear-rings the girl wore, and she pouted but removed them.

'Lips,' he demanded next, and she pursed up her mouth to him and he rubbed a tissue across.

'Can I keep my eyes, Uncle Huw?' she begged. 'They have to be removed carefully. That's true, isn't it?' She looked for help from Manny.

'True,' Manny nodded. 'I'd leave her to cream them off if I were you.'

'Women!' Huw Grant snorted.

He started the engine again, but did not move off at once.

'Manny Norbert, this is my niece Jane Mackie. For heaven's sake settle yourself, Jane, before your ex-head changes her mind and decides to keep you after all.'

Jane laughed. 'She won't, she's as glad to be free of me as I'm glad to be free of school. I'm never going to another lesson.'

'You're going to a lot of lessons. You're enrolling at the Elkington High as soon as the new term begins.' Huw released the brake.

'Elkington?' queried Jane.

'It's in the hinterland behind Soleil Bay. You're not up here just to surf and sun-bake, Jane.'

'But, Uncle Huw——'

'You're only fifteen——'

'Fifteen and a half.'

'And you'll take a school bus into Elkington every school morning and get the school bus back again.'

There was silence for a few moments. Then:

'You said a high school, not a Saint Something,' Jane checked.

'Yes.'

'Possibly a co-ed?'

Manny, who had attended Elkington High herself, supplied: 'Yes, it is co-ed.'

'Mmm!' smiled Jane.

Huw Grant flicked one of his quick looks at Manny, but she pretended not to see.

They had lunch at one of the Pacific Highway towns, then turned east along the rough road that led to the bay.

'It's being sealed,' Huw Grant advised Manny. 'It should have been done in the beginning, but apparently it was overlooked. Now it's needed as soon as possible, as the rutile yield is rising.'

'None of us wanted any road improvements,' Manny said, 'we wanted the old place left as it is.'

'It will be,' he assured her. 'I'm restoration-slanted.'

'But with a new road people will come.'

'Of course, but pages have to be turned. *You* have found that.'

Jane, listening avidly at the back, sensing some drama somewhere, broke in: 'What did you find when you turned a page, Miss Norbert? Please can I call you Manny?'

'Of course, Jane, but there was no page, so nothing was found. Mr Grant is merely imagining.'

'Huw,' he reminded her. 'Like you, Jane, Manny doesn't respond to instruction.'

'Good,' welcomed Jane, glad of a fellow spirit. Her blue glance fell on the blue dress. 'Wow!' she admired. 'Was this to be the gown in the page Uncle Huw was talking about, Manny? Was the page a wedding? Were you going to be married? Who to? When? Did he stop it? Didn't you marry after all? What happened? Oh, it's a lovely dress! I'd like to——'

'Then you can,' said Manny.

'No, she can't,' Huw came in. 'Put it down and behave yourself. We're coming to the camp. But *you* won't be sleeping there, Jane, it's strictly, emphatically men only. Do you hear me?'

'Yes, Uncle Huw, but where will I sleep, then?'

'In the Norbert cottage which practically adjoins.' He looked promptingly at Manny, and Manny bit her lip but did not disagree even though she resented not being told this first.

'Strictly men,' Jane echoed of the camp. 'All old like you, Uncle Huw? No, there's a young one.' She peered out with satisfaction. It was Umberto, Manny saw, one of the high school vacation intake, for the project did that every end of semester, a very likeable Italian boy.

'You see,' marked Huw in a low voice.

But Manny only smiled; she knew Umberto and was unconcerned. She began gathering her things. However, when Huw pulled up at the Norbert bungalow she gave Jane the key and told her to go ahead.

'You look for trouble,' she warned Huw as she accepted her bag from him.'

'By bringing her here? Yes, I know that.'

'No, I meant that significant look you gave me. Umberto is a lamb.'

'With a wolf underneath?'

'Don't be so suspicious!'

'Very well, but I'll still be looking at you if anything happens.'

'You didn't tell me I was to be a child-keeper,' she said crossly.

'You're not, just an eye on her and a report to me will do. After all, you're being very well treated, aren't you, being allowed to cancel a debt with no pressure put on you to speed up the process while we wait.' He looked hard at her and Manny seethed, but did not disagree.

'All right then, I'll watch her ... but you watch your own domain, watch your old sand-mining.'

'And you refrain from watching the sand-miners. Lightning can strike twice.'

'If you're referring to Justin, he was a clerk, not a miner.'

'Yes. The accounts.' He got back into the car and drove to the adjoining camp.

What an objectionable man he was, Manny thought, yet his niece Jane, precocious though she might be, seemed quite likeable.

She climbed the verandah steps, for a moment forgetting her troubles as she remembered back to when the cottage grounds extended right down to the sea. Now the mining project came between, its ugly apparatus and hideous upheaval spoiling the view, though one day it would all go, everything return to what it once was. But did things ever go back or did they only go forward, like pages turned forward and not back? She entered the house and exclaimed at once:

'Jane!'

For Jane was standing there in the blue dress, bright golden hair doing more for it, Manny thought ruefully, than her own tow would have, cornflower eyes more than pickle.

'I shouldn't have,' Jane said apologetically, 'but it's so beautiful. I'm a tight fit, I know, but——' She pivoted around.

'Come away from the window,' appealed Manny, 'or your uncle——'

'Oh, yes, poor Uncle Huw. He'll tell me again how I take after Judy.'

'Judy?' Manny queried.

'The rash one,' said Jane. 'Can I keep it on for a little while longer, Manny?'

'Until I unpack, then,' Manny conceded, and went on to her room. She hung up her things, tidied her hair, then came out to find Jane and suggest a cup of coffee.

Jane was not there. She looked around the other rooms but still could not see her.

There was a narrow track rimming the fence of the rutile to permit public access to the sea, perhaps Jane had taken that. Manny went down the track. She was picking her way over it, and feeling very

inadequate losing her charge this soon, when a flash
of colour caught her eye. Blue. She stopped.

Inside the fence, not out as she should be, Jane,
ostensibly enquiring sensibly about the workings of
some machinery but really not looking at all, looking
instead at the boy Umberto, trilled a sweet laugh.
Umberto, instantly won over, and who wouldn't be
with Jane's richer build and brighter colouring,
laughed back. Jane was positively irresistible, Manny
thought, no wonder Huw Grant——

'Jane!' she called sharply.

'Coming, Manny. Manny, this is Umberto. Umberto, this is——'

'We already know each other,' Manny broke in
sternly.

She hurried Jane back to the cottage, glad that no
one else had been there, that no one else had seen.

Her relief was shortlived. Huw Grant stood on
the verandah as they came up the path.

'Have you unpacked your bags, Jane?' he asked.
'Do so now. Also' ... indubitably noting Jane's young
over-curves ... '*take off that dress.*'

He turned to Manny as Jane turned to obey, then
gave an imperative indicative nod in the direction
of the sea, a gesture Manny could not possibly mis-
understand. She hesitated, then, hating herself but
knowing she had to do it, complied.

Together they walked down to the beach.

CHAPTER FOUR

IT had always been a beautiful beach, silken-sanded, crystal-watered, untenanted because of its rough road from Elkington Town. Now with road improvement all that would alter, the tranquillity would be challenged, the Elkington cars would come racing out every week-end to participate in the pleasures of the coast, everything would be spoiled.

Manny stood gazing at her beloved shoreline while she waited for Huw Grant's censure, since undoubtedly he had seen where Jane had come from. Mentally, meanwhile, she composed a few pertinent retorts of her own; she was determined not to be too cast down. She found it hard, though, for her attention kept wandering to the washing shells she had loved to gather as a child, to the fat jelly boys, to the silver sound of the swirl and withdrawal of the cream-tipped waves. It was all too beautiful for anger, she decided, but try to tell that to Mr Huw Grant. King Grant.

To her surprise, though, Huw Grant started on another theme.

'Did your father disclose what he intended to paint into the mural?' he asked.

'...Not fully,' Manny said with hidden shame. She had been arguing at that incubation period of Dad's, protesting over Justin, she had been self-absorbed and not listening to any words but her own.

'It was a restoration motif,' she heard Huw saying. 'Your father wanted to convey man giving back to the damaged soil, the soil giving back to the trees, the trees giving back to the first beginnings of things. Complete cycle. I suggested naming it "Return to Love" ... even "Come back to Love." What do you think?'

'Come back to Love ... oh, yes, that's right.' Quite compulsively Manny heard herself agreeing, for the name indeed *was* right. She glanced a little startled at her fingertips, for there was a tingling in them. She felt a sudden urge to race up to her father's studio to take up a brush.

Huw Grant was looking at her with a knowledge that she would have resented had she not been so caught up. First the shoreline as it once was, she was picturing, then man's monstrous interference, then—— Come back to Love.

'You see,' Huw Grant broke in, 'you were intended to remain here. Emmanuelle Norbert, to take up where Hal Norbert left off.'

Her fingertips were normalising now, her senses returning.

'I haven't Dad's ability,' she said as she had said before.

'But you'll try.'

'I might try a very long time.'

'There's no hurry.' He looked meaningly back at the mechanical sand monsters not nearly ready to leave the scene yet. 'Meanwhile you could see out the lease, make preliminary sketches, even paint a picture if you felt like it. Then with what I pay you for Jane——'

'Pay me for Jane?' Manny looked surprised. 'But you distinctly said——'

'Yes, I know I said that you were well recompensed by my not asking you yet for the advance to be returned, but I hadn't realized what a charge Jane could be, not until I watched her walk up that path just now in your too-tight blue dress. Then, Manny' ... a firming of already firm lips ... 'I did realise. At once I decided to put everything on a proper footing.'

'Yes?'

'You're to be paid for keeping an eye on Jane. No, I am adamant about that.'

'But that's silly,' Manny objected, 'if it's sleeping at the cottage instead of the camp that you mean, for there's plenty of room.'

'It's not what I mean, though I must apologise for springing that imposition on you. I hadn't remembered until we actually arrived here how male a male camp is, and how female——' He shrugged. 'No, Manny, it's more than that, more than a house instead of a camp, it's Jane herself. So I intend to pay you the same as Jane's parents have been paying her school.'

'But she was taught at school,' Manny pointed out.

'You'll be teaching her.'

'Art? Jane wants to paint?'

'You'll be teaching her to grow up.'

'*I* teach her? Haven't you changed your mind? Before you said——'

'Yes, I said you were of marriageable age but not yet a woman.'

'You added that you were not, of course, Justin Welsh,' she said in a low voice.

'That's true. I told you I hadn't noticed any womanhood, but now ...'

He stood looking at her, looking at the young woman breasts pushing softly yet strongly against the simple cotton of her T-shirt, and his silver eyes said something else.

Manny flushed vividly under his scrutiny, unaware that in her embarrassment she had blossomed perceptibly, only aware of a man's eyes on her in a way she had never experienced before. With Justin she had never felt like this in spite of all the rather questionable, or so she had inwardly considered, things he had said to her.

She could think of nothing to say.

'Emmanuelle, do you know you're beautiful?' Huw broke in unexpectedly.

'What, tow and pickle?' Manny was taken by surprise.

'You're beautiful,' he repeated.

'I'm not, but your niece is.'

'Yes, and I'd like to keep her a beautiful *child*. At least until her parents return.'

'Is that the deal, then?' Manny asked him. 'A child not a woman?'

He grinned at her astuteness. 'Is it too difficult?'

'It's difficult, but I don't think too difficult. Already I like Jane very much. But can you tell me something about her?'

'She's an only child,' he obliged.

'What else?'

'Precocious, but not hopelessly so, I think.'

'I think, too. She described herself as rash.'

'That rather surprises me, knowing Jane's bird brain I suspect rash to her means something like measles.' He laughed, but Manny found she could not laugh with him.

'She said she took after Judy, the rash one,' she went on. She looked at him and waited, but he did not reply.

'Anything else?' Manny asked at last.

'Nothing.' The answer came quite harshly, and Manny saw that he had turned away and was preparing to return to the camp. After a moment of puzzlement at the abrupt end to a discussion that had barely begun, Huw Grant climbing over the wire enclosure back to his headquarters by this time, Manny went up the track to the house.

Jane had found the iron, smoothed the blue dress and put it on a hanger she had also found.

'I'm good at domestic things,' she said as Manny thanked her, 'things to do with your hands. I'd make a good hairdresser, but most of all, if I could only pass the exam, I'd like to be a nurse.'

Nursing reminded Manny of the abrupt end to her meeting with Huw on the beach. It was hard to pinpoint the actual termination of their conversation, but she felt sure it had come after she had mentioned Judy, the rash one, as described by Jane. Huw seemed to have clammed up from then on.

'Nursing is an art as well as a calling, Jane,' she said to the girl. 'For instance, you have to know why as well as how.'

'Why what?' asked Jane.

'Why a bandage? Why a medicine? Why—a rash?' It was a tedious approach, but Manny felt she could scarcely ask a fifteen-year-old: 'Do you really know what's meant by rash?'

'A bandage for an injury, a medicine for an illness, a rash from measles,' Jane said airily.

Measles was what Huw had smiled, Manny remembered, adding that his niece's bird brain would only associate rash with that, yet when Manny had mentioned Judy, the rash one, there had been a very different effect on Huw. He had turned and left Manny standing on the beach.

'Who is Judy?' she asked directly, no more roundabout approaches.

'Oh, one of those people that get popped out regularly by adults who don't think you're listening. Like Tommy takes after Grandpa, or Gloria resembles Grandma. I, it seems, am Judy.'

'But who is Judy? Judy, the rash one?'

'An aunt, Manny, and I'm her all over again, or so I hear when I shouldn't hear. I've decided it must be the temperamental rash they mean, not the measles, as I've never had measles,' Jane laughed.

Proving one point, Manny said to herself, Jane is *not* a bird brain.

'You shouldn't have gone into the camp, Jane.' She changed the subject. 'Your uncle told you that.'

'He only said I didn't sleep there, so how was I to know? Anyway, we'll have to go over there tonight, there's nothing to eat in the house. I've been snooping around, I'm a very good cook, but there's nothing to work on. So the canteen it is.' Jane glowed.

But if Jane glowed, Manny groaned. She knew Huw Grant would not like that at all. She had forgotten she had diminished her supplies when she had gone down to Sydney.

'I'll run over to the company store and buy something,' she said.

'Can I come, too?'

'Definitely no. You stay outside, Jane. Your uncle said that.'

'His words were men only,' pouted Jane, 'and you're going.'

'I'm old, and I've always gone.'

'All right then,' Jane accepted gloomily. 'I can see this is going to be fun ... like fun!'

Manny ran over to the shop where she knew supplies were always on sale. She bought tins of salmon and fruit and a slab of cake. As she came out again she saw Jane emerging from the office in spite of what she had told her. She went across.

'Jane——' she began, but Jane was ready for her.

'The office isn't entirely inside, it's also outside. Inside would mean completely within the fence, but the office is not.'

'You know what I meant, and what your uncle meant,' reproved Manny, but seeing that actually Jane was right, that the office was free of the wire on the road side but inside the enclosure on the project side, she let it pass.

'Yes, I do know, Manny, and I'm sorry about it now, because it rather spoiled things for me. It spoiled Umberto.'

'What do you mean, Jane?'

'There wasn't anyone in the office, so I waited for a while. You see' ... demurely ... 'I'm very interested in minerals and sand-mining.'

'Go on, Jane,' said Manny.

'But no one came, so I just ... idly ... turned over a book on the desk. It was called Work Personnel.'

'Just idly you chose Work Personnel,' disbelieved Manny.

'I wanted to find out Umberto's second name. But I wish I hadn't. Manny, he's the same age as I am. Worse still—he's younger. I'm rising sixteen, fifteen and a half is sixteen, and he's three months younger than me. Oh, Manny!'

'Why, yes, Jane, Umberto is at Elkington High. The firm takes on boys during vacation, hoping they'll like the job and apply for a cadetship later.'

'Fifteen!' groaned Jane. 'Everything fell to pieces at once.'

Manny tried not to laugh at her, but it was hard, and she had to turn away. 'I got salmon,' she said brightly, 'could our cook concoct something out of that?'

'I could make salmon soufflé, salmon au gratin, salmon croquettes,' welcomed Jane, her disappointment forgotten.

It was only when the meal was over that she spoke of the episode again.

'Umberto Gino Fuccilli,' she sighed. 'Fifteen. Not even and a half like I am.' She was thoughtful a moment. 'Manny——'

'Yes, Jane?'

'After my bitter disappointment over Umberto I spent some time looking at the other names.'

'And ages,' added Manny with a smile.

'Well, yes, I did that, and most of them are as old as Uncle Huw. But the last name ... well, I'm sure I've heard of it before. Who was he, do you know? Is he still here?'

'Really, Jane, how can I say if you don't——' Manny stopped herself. The last name, Jane had just said. Would that be—alphabetically W was far down on the list.

'Justin Welsh. Isn't Justin gorgeous? Really romantic, don't you think? But Manny, where have I heard it before? Justin Welsh?'

'Possibly you've read something like it in a magazine story,' Manny suggested, 'it rather has that kind of sound.' She said it hopefully.

'You mean hero sound,' nodded Jane, 'yes, it has. Or it might be the name of a movie star. We used to smuggle movie mags into the class—they were taboo, you see.'

'Or a TV actor,' Manny proffered, relieved that Jane was easy to divert, but wishing she could also divert herself. For the moment Justin's name had come up she had started thinking about him. There had not been much opportunity before, but now he came clearly to her, blue-eyed, charming ... very charming. She remembered a little wistfully how well they had always got on together, how magic it had been those few days when she had gone down to Sydney and he had suddenly appeared. She wondered whether if Huw Grant had not come along with his forceful interference, if Justin had turned up as planned, if she had not had that eleventh-hour change of mind, she would have regained the magic. If a mangled beach could come back to beauty surely two people could go on from where they had left off and find something as well.

'Manny, what's a mural?' Jane was asking. 'Oh, I know it's a very large picture on a wall, but a *mural*?'

'Most murals have a theme, Jane—they tell, or try to tell, a story. The mural your uncle has commissioned for his company will describe Soleil Bay as it was in the beginning, its chaos later because of the mining, finally its restoration.'

'That sounds a hard job,' Jane commented.

'It will be,' Manny said with feeling.

'I wish I could help you,' Jane told Manny. 'I shall, of course, by taking over the housekeeping.' She looked enquiringly at Manny, and Manny smiled back at her.

'Thank you, Jane, that will be a wonderful gesture.' She spoke sincerely, for the meal the girl had produced had convinced her that Jane was a very capable young woman.

But Jane was still unsatisfied with herself. 'I wish I could help more, Manny.'

'You can, you can wash the brushes for me, help me mix the paints. Also' ... with inspiration ... 'you can keep a look out for likely items to include in the mural, say a certain tree that catches your eye, a bush that strikes you, perhaps a particular aspect of the beach. My first commitment is Soleil Bay as it was before the sand-mining invasion, so I'll be needing that kind of stuff.'

'But if it's to be as it was, how can I look for it now?'

'Good question,' Manny nodded. 'We'll look further away where the mining has not yet begun its damage. I'll reconstruct from that.'

After the meal was over the two girls washed the dishes together, then, a little nervously, Manny walked to the studio and opened the door. There were canvases on the easels, canvases on the floor, some covered with sheets, some bare.

'Are any of them yours?' Jane had followed Manny.

Manny nodded to one of the walls, for she was too choked up to speak. She was standing by the commissioned mural now, it used up the entire eastern wall. It had been lovingly set up, the working material laid carefully out, an initial wash applied to the first section, but that was as far as it had gone. She took up a brush resting on a palette and held it gently. This would be the first time it had been taken up since Dad had put it down. Finally down. Her touch on the brush was tender.

'Shall I clean it for you?' Jane asked eagerly.

'Not this one,' Manny said. She held it tightly for several moments, then put it in her pocket.

Jane wandered around the room for a while, picking things up, putting them back, then, evidently bored, she went out again. Presently Manny heard the record player turning, so, assured that Jane was occupied, not trespassing where she had been directed not to, she turned her attention to the mural again.

She decided to start with the headland. She would sweep the hill down to the sea and in the long grassy slope she planned to introduce a lot of the things that she had loved as a child. The Lightning Tree, for instance, a tall coast gum that lightning had once struck but never killed, for it had come together again from two distinct segments, and grown up whole and strong.

Then there was the stream that spilled over, that after rain formed a silver fall. The little hollow half-way down where buttercups grew. Suddenly excited, Manny made a few light pencil guidemarks on the mural. She would have the tree there, the stream here, the hollow——

It was half an hour before she realised that the music had stopped, that the house was in silence.

Jane, she thought guiltily. She put the pencil down and went out.

The record player was going round and round. Jane must have left before the record was finished. Where had she gone?

In her anxiety to catch the girl up before her uncle saw her, Manny blundered straight out of the cottage into someone's arms.

'You're in a hurry,' a voice said.

It was Huw Grant, and Manny could have cried with frustration. She trusted Jane, she didn't think Jane—— But she still did not *know*.

'Well, Emmanuelle?' He was standing looking down at her. It was evening now, but still early evening, and the rather pale dusk as yet highlighted his too-etched, still youngish face.

'I——' But Manny hesitated, not because she did not know what to say but because when she had stumbled into him he had steadied her, and after the steadying had not removed one of his hands. The hand was supporting her shoulder, but part of his long forefinger was still on her breast. She felt her heart beating under the finger and wondered if he was feeling the beat, too.

'Did you want something?' she asked.

'Yes. I've learned that you were over at the store earlier.'

'To buy our tea. There was nothing in the house, and I knew you wouldn't want us to eat there, so I bought something instead,' she said nervously.

The quiver in her voice did not escape him. 'You make me sound like a jailer,' he reproached. 'I'm not. Don't make too much of an issue of any restriction or you'll have Jane a martyr, and martyrdom can be dangerous.' He looked meaningly at her, and she was aware to what he referred. She was also sharply aware that he had still not removed his hand.

She wanted to step back, but that would have created an emphasis on that hand, so she stood, waiting for him to break away first.

'Where's Jane?' he asked casually, and Manny tried to answer casually.

'She was playing records.'

He caught that instantly. '...Was?'

'I was in the studio, and then the music stopped.' In her concern this time Manny did step away, and with the finger gone all her barely held composure fell apart. 'Oh, where can she be?' she cried.

'Have you looked?'

'No.'

'Have you called her?'

'No.'

'Then good grief, Manny, stop over-reacting. Do I frighten you as much as that, as much as being scared to death even before an event?'

'Y-yes, yes, you do.'

'Then we'll have to do something about that, won't we? But first of all we'll find Jane.'

He went into the house.

Manny came behind him, annoyed with herself that she had not done this first, had not paused even to cancel the record player, as he was doing now ... laughing as he did. For on the floor beside the player, but concealed at a first glance because in her sleep she had rolled slightly away, lay Jane. Even as Manny looked down she gave a little snore.

'Tuckered out.' There was a smile in Huw Grant's voice. 'Get a pillow and a rug and we'll leave her there.'

'But she can't——'

'Yes, she can, kids can sleep anywhere. This cushion will do, ease up her head.'

Jane grunted as they slid the cushion under her, then put a warm rug over her, but she never woke.

'Now you,' Huw said when they had finished, 'shall I put you to bed as well?'

'Unlike Jane, I'm not tuckered.' Manny moved out to the verandah so as not to disturb the girl.

With almost incredible quickness he was behind her, compelling her round to him before she knew what he was doing.

'Then if you're not tired we'll have that lesson, I think.'

'Lesson?' she queried.

'That teaching you not to be scared of me, Manny. Shall we start with—this?'

At once he was kissing her, light, inconsequential kisses on the lift of her brows, and then, still light, on each eyelid. Next she felt his warm breath close to her ear-tips, and wondered why she was standing still like this when she so wholeheartedly disliked him, waiting for another kiss. A kiss on her lips.

She heard him laughing softly, teasing her. 'That's enough instruction for tonight,' he said, and he put his long forefinger, the finger that had rested earlier on her breast, lightly but with unmistakable promise on her mouth.

'More lessons later,' he said softly. 'Sleep now.'

And Manny heard him cross to the camp.

CHAPTER FIVE

MANNY was up early the next morning. She did not pause even to brew a quick cup, instead she put on her old painting smock, and, tiptoeing so as not to disturb Jane, she went along to the studio. She had wakened with a tingle in her fingers and an idea in her head. Teetering Rock—she must find room to paint in Teetering Rock.

Teetering Rock had been a favourite spot of hers ever since childhood. It comprised a strong rock platform rising squarely up from the headland, then horizontally across its flat top another slimmer rock. This second rock, delicately balanced, actually teetered in a strong wind, and for safety's sake should have been blasted away years ago, but since no one came here, since no one bothered, Teetering Rock had survived. Manny had always been strictly warned about it, and obediently never went near it, but she still loved it and felt it must go into the mural. She took her pencil, contemplated the canvas, then made a small indicative mark for its inclusion. After Jane awakened and they breakfasted they would go up to the headland and she would sketch old Teetering Rock.

As though she had heard Manny's thoughts, Jane walked in at that moment, crushed and touselled from sleeping on the floor, but otherwise unaffected.

'I died,' she grinned. 'Are you painting already?'

'No, I'm waiting for you to produce something to eat, Jane, but' ... with a sudden sheepish look ... 'I don't know what. I never thought about breakfast yesterday when I bought our supper.'

'Well, evidently someone thought, because there are eggs and bacon on the kitchen table. Uncle Huw must have brought them.'

'No, he didn't, he——' Manny stopped. He didn't, she knew, because he couldn't have been carrying

them since both his arms had been steadying someone, and one finger——

'Probably he sent someone over, then. Could even
have been Junior.'

'Junior?'

'The fifteen-year-old,' Jane scoffed. 'I'll fix breakfast, Manny.'

She did it expertly, and Manny ate with relish. She
asked Jane would she like to come out on a material-
gathering expedition, and Jane said she would.

They decided to make a picnic of it, and while
Manny gathered pencils and drawing blocks, Jane
made sandwiches and filled a flask.

They took the cliff track that led southward and
upward from the project's titanium section and were
soon above, though still in sight of, the camp. It was
a flawless morning, the sea a shining blue, and where
the sun fell on the jutting rocks it changed the dark
honey of the stone to warm red.

Jane began singing, and Manny, excited because
the tingling in her fingertips was starting again,
began sketching eagerly, here an unusual tree, there
a striking bush. She lost sight of Jane.

She was in a world of her own when the scream
penetrated her absorption. There was no doubting
that scream, it held sheer, unspeakable terror. Manny
dropped the pad to the ground at once and ran.

She had not seen Jane for some time, but had
thought nothing of it, for whatever else Jane was she
certainly had shown no athletic, adventurous ten-
dencies. Yet, reaching the source of the scream, there
was Jane on Teetering Rock.

The girl must have been eager to show her what

she had found for the mural, not knowing that it was for the rock that they had come, then decided that it would make it even more spectacular if she climbed and demonstrated it. How such an inexperienced girl had got where she had, Manny did not know, but eagerness could do a lot, and Jane had certainly managed to scale right up. Remembering she had not been warned about the second rock, Manny's look climbed fearfully to where Jane perforce had stopped, and that was the extreme top. Jane had even clambered on to the cross rock, the teetering rock that swayed on a high wind.

It was not swaying now, though, and that was not what was frightening the ashen Jane, it was the distance, unrealised by her before, to the ground.

'Manny,' she called, seeing her, 'I didn't think it was this high. Now I can't get down!'

'I don't want you to come down, I don't want you to move.'

'Manny——'

'Stop there while I get in sight of the camp and scream, while I wave distress. *Stop*, Jane!'

'I can't. Manny, Manny, come back!' For Manny was flying to a break in the cliff's bushes through which some of the taller mining machinery and its attendant workers was visible. She began yelling and waving her arms. She kept on doing it ... she felt her voice would break, her arms fall off ... until she saw a movement from someone in one of the loaders. Somebody had heard and then seen her and was waving back. That was all she needed. She returned to Jane.

Now she could see the rock moving, very slightly,

but a teetering had certainly begun. The movement was accentuated by Jane's movement, for the girl was shifting unconsciously in her deep fear, not keeping still as she had been told. As Manny watched she saw one end of the rock slightly seesaw.

'Jane,' she called, 'keep as quiet as you can. *Please*, Jane. Jane' ... the seesaw accelerating ... 'I'm coming up!'

She had never climbed Teetering Rock before, the rock had been strictly for viewing, not climbing, but if Jane, younger but bulkier, could do it, then age but less weight certainly must. Manny threw off her shoes and began to scale up in her bare feet.

The rock surface cut her abominably, but at least she was afforded better toeholds. She felt her fingernails tearing, but she did not care, she saw she was reaching the top. Now came the tricky part, the decision on where to haul herself so as to counterbalance Jane. Allowing for Jane being heavier should she——

'To the left!' Huw Grant called from underneath her. She glanced quickly down and saw him there with a group of men.

'Look up,' he called sharply, 'not down. Neither of you move. Do you hear that, Jane?'

Jane only sobbed.

He waited a moment, then he called: 'We've got to get you off immediately, a wind is springing up. We can't come up for you, it would be disastrous, so you'll have to jump.'

Jane screamed at once: 'I can't jump!'

'But first,' went on Huw, ignoring Jane, 'you must

balance or it will all be over before you can do anything about it. Manny, move a few inches more to the left ... the *left*, I said.

'Now I'm going to count to three. It's a high jump but a fairly reasonable one. All you'll get is a shaking-up. Jane, are you heeding?

'There's a net waiting, it's a strong, safe one. The men will catch you. You'll have nothing to worry about. Jane first, then when I call a moment after, you, Manny. But before that you must move up another inch for counterbalance. Now get cracking, Manny.'

'Yes,' said Manny, and she moved up.

'Count,' she called presently, hoping the sickness she felt was not evident in her quavering voice, for she was beginning to twitch, and even that could start the rock's premature fall.

'No, don't count,' Jane screamed, 'I can't jump, I just can't!' She took an instinctive step forward to Manny as though for comfort, and the rock began to dip from each end in turn, the movements becoming deeper and faster.

'*Push* her, Manny!' Huw's voice cut through Manny's terror as Jane came a step closer. For a moment Manny paused, then Huw called again, willing her, *forcing* her, and bending over from the waist, not daring to put a foot forward, Manny pushed the girl. At once, with the loss of Jane's weight as Jane hurtled down, the rock shot upward and Manny crashed downward herself.

She was caught by a pair of arms, not a net, and the arms and their owner descended to the ground with her. There she was covered by his body, and pressed down until the rock had crashed, and it was safe to get up.

Manny looked giddily skyward. The cross rock had fallen on the other side, and the men who had caught Jane between them were putting her on her feet. There was no net after all, the men had formed their own refuge with their entwined arms, so what Huw had called must have only been called in encouragement.

'Is Jane——' Manny tried to ask.

'She's all right,' Huw assured her. 'What about you?'

'I'm fine, I'm——'

Manny said no more, instead she slid down to the ground again.

When she came to she was in her bed at the bungalow. She was washed and in her nightdress and the blind was drawn.

It took her some time to focus properly, and when she did she saw that someone was sitting in a chair beside the bed. After some more focusing she saw it was Huw Grant.

'You?' she exclaimed in surprise.

'You're supposed to say "Where am I?" first,' he reminded her.

'I'm in my own bed. But how?'

'We carried you back, of course. Did you think we were going to leave you there?'

'I suppose it was a temptation,' she admitted.

'A big one, but it just isn't done.'

'Did I pass out?'

'Yes.'

'And Jane? ... But Jane must be all right, otherwise I wouldn't be here like this.' Dear, efficient Jane, Manny appreciated, she had not only put her into her nightdress but she had most thoroughly cleansed and bandaged her first.

'Jane is in her room, too. Like you, she's suffering from the after-effects.'

'Jane is——' Manny sat up, trying to force her fuddled mind to work out a few things. Like being dressed in a nightgown. Like being bathed and bandaged as she was. Like——

Huw Grant sat patiently while she did so.

'Did Jane——' Manny asked at length, but found she could not finish it. As no question had been asked, he could not reply, so she began again. 'Did you send to Elkington for a nurse?'

'For cut toes, no,' he replied scornfully, 'for that's all you've suffered, and Jane even less. But you both got a shaking up, as I said you would, but as you had the greater trauma of pushing Jane off, jumping last, we'll allow you the privilege of fainting.'

'Thank you,' Manny accepted nervously.

She was silent a while, then she tried to probe him.

'I expect Jane,' she said cunningly, 'not having passed out came home and—and fixed me up, then went to bed herself.'

'No,' he said again.

'... Then——?'

This time Manny did focus clearly, and looked at him in direct enquiry. Surely *he* hadn't ... no, she was sure he wouldn't ...

Smiling amiably, Huw Grant adjusted the top sheet

of Manny's bed like any good nurse.

'I did it,' he said.

'Oh.' What else could she say? Manny thought.

Hatefully Huw Grant gave her ample time to think of something, then when it became apparent that she had no words he went outside to return very soon with tea.

Manny drank it eagerly; as well as being thirsty she could hide part of her flushed face in the cup.

'I'm blowing the rock up,' Huw told her, drinking tea himself. 'It's a hazard.'

'Can I include it in the mural, though? It has a fascinating look, I always think.'

'It's your work,' he shrugged.

'But has to be approved by you.'

'Then sketch it in roughly and I'll tell you then. Now I'm going to leave you to sleep.'

'I don't want to sleep.'

'You will, though,' he smiled shrewdly, and took up her cup before she could examine it for evidence, then went out.

I do believe he put a sedative in it, Manny seethed. She knew he had some hours later, but it didn't matter then, she felt new and fresh and ready to begin again ... that was except when she remembered——

She resolved to put all that aside. She got up and dressed. She was fit everywhere save her feet. Looking down, she saw that they were well swathed in bandages, so her cuts must have been extensive.

She hobbled out to the studio, she wanted to etch in Teetering Rock while it was still clear in her mind. When she got to the doorway she stood staring in unwilling gratitude. Huw ... it would have to be him ... had fixed it so that she could sit as she worked. Her toes thanked him for that.

She sketched in the rock, the Lightning Tree, a few other things that had struck her, then she sat back and half-closed her eyes on the big canvas. Something was emerging, she saw with a thrill.

From the kitchen she heard voices, and curiously she hobbled out to see who was there. Jane was in one of her aprons and Umberto was in another. The two children, for what else were they? were stirring something at the stove.

For a moment Manny stood smiling, then she remembered her position, and wiped the smile off.

'Jane!' she called.

Jane turned round happily, no guilt at all.

'How are you, Manny? Uncle Huw sent over more supplies with Umberto and said Umberto could stay to help me with them. He must think I can't cook.'

Umberto broke in: 'Which she can.'

'And *he* can.' No longer was Jane demeaning fifteen-year-olds with no extra half to diminish that shame, she was very impressed. 'We're having ravioli, Manny,' she said, 'proper ravioli, not from a tin.'

'I see.' Manny didn't, but if Huw Grant chose to allow what he had instructed her not to allow, then it was on his shoulders.

Broad shoulders. She thought this as the shoulders and the man came up the path to her.

'You're up,' he called.

'How long did you expect?'

'Exactly as long as it's taken, I worked your medi-

cine out before I administered it. No, don't look indignant about it, you needed to be wound down.'

'Well, seeing Jane and Umberto doubled up over
one saucepan wound me up again,' Manny retorted.

'But I did it on your recommendation, remember?
You told me I looked for trouble.'

'Don't tell me you listen to what I say,' she said
sarcastically.

'Surprise?' he baited. He nodded in the direction
of the kitchen. 'There was,' he admitted, 'another
reason. It's Umberto himself. He can't clerk for nuts,
and never will.'

'Then engineering?'

'Worse still. Yet his parents are determined he
won't do as his father does, as his grandfather did.
As Umberto wants to.'

'Cook?'

'Yes,' said Huw. 'They asked me to try him in the
school vacation intake. Well' ... a shrug ... 'I've
tried.'

'I take it your report won't be favourable.'

'I don't know yet,' Huw grinned, 'I haven't tasted
the canneloni.'

'It's going to be ravioli. Is that why you came, to
check the children?'

'Also you. I wanted to see if you'd emerged.'

'I have,' she assured him.

'Good, then, because you're having a visitor. Larry
was at the drama this morning, though you wouldn't
have seen him. Now he wants to visit you, satisfy
himself you're in one piece. He seems to think a lot
of you.'

'We've known each other a long time. Unlike the others he was not brought in with the rutile team, he was a local. I'm very fond of Larry.'

'All the boys are as well,' observed Huw.

'. . . And the boss?' Manny probed.

'Now that's more difficult. Larry is the company's chip on the shoulder, the dissenting voice. Every outfit has one.'

'The men must have a representative,' she pointed out.

'Of course, and I could have a worse one than Larry. But until the Welsh business dies down . . .'

'I thought it had died.'

'It's not quite dead yet, but it will be. I just thought I'd warn you, Manny, that Larry might bring up the subject of Justin Welsh. Best for you to be prepared, then it might not hurt so much.'

'But it wouldn't hur——' Manny stopped herself. 'Thanks for the consideration,' she said instead.

Huw nodded, stopped for a few minutes longer, then went back to the camp. He had scarcely closed his office door which was visible from the cottage than Larry came across.

Larry sat on the botom verandah step and Manny sat on the top.

'We all reckon you scared us this morning, Manny,' said Larry. 'It was bad enough losing our old man without losing our young Manny soon after.'

'Well, you didn't lose her,' Manny said cheerfully. 'How are things?'

'Hard to tell. I haven't worked him out yet.'

'You mean the new boss?'

'Yes.'

'What about the boys?'

'Well, Peter was more easy-going,' Larry reminded her.

'And often not going at all,' Manny defended for Huw. She was surprised with herself. 'The camp was a disgrace.'

'The work wasn't as regimented,' Larry argued.

'All the same, I had a peep at the mess when I was over there yesterday, and I think you're being done like kings.'

'Pay envelopes, too. This new fellow is finding us overtime.'

'So what is it?' Manny probed. 'I can see it's something.'

'It's Welsh, Manny. The way he was got rid of.'

'That's weeks ago now.'

'But it still worries me. I never liked Welsh, but you know me.'

'Oh, yes, I know you, always for the underdog.' As she said it Manny thought wryly that she had never seen anyone less like an underdog than Justin.

'Nothing made public,' went on Larry in a concerned voice, 'that was what got me. At least I'd like to *know*.'

'About Justin Welsh?'

'Yes, Manny. Oh, I've heard the men talking about his books not quite balancing, but a fellow doesn't get what Grant gave him for that, not without getting a fair go first.'

'He got a fair go, Larry,' she insisted.

'Handed over to the law!'

'But he wasn't.'

'Then why didn't Grant say so? Why did he let us all think he was?'

'Discipline?' suggested Manny.

'Yes, he'd have plenty of that. Well, young Manny, I'm glad you're only wounded in your toes. Keep your shoes on next time.' Larry rumpled Manny's hair affectionately, then left.

But at the gate he turned again. 'How do you know all this?'

'Huw ... Mr Grant told me. And Larry, believe me, it's *for sure.*' Of course it was for sure, Manny knew, Justin had been let off on the condition he did not turn up at a church, and he had not.

'Oh.' Larry looked interested. 'Is *that* how it is, and we all thought that you and Welsh ... Well, after all, you were acting a bit thick together. Yet all the time it was ... or will be ... Hi there, young Manny!' For Manny, forgetting her feet, had descended the steps to throw a pebble at him.

The pebble missed Larry, but it caught Huw Grant, who was crossing to the cottage once more. Larry laughed delightedly, probably the first breakdown between him and the new boss.

'He'll tell the whole outfit,' said Huw, reaching Manny's side. 'Well, what did our shop steward have to say?'

'Is it Larry you've come about?'

'Look, I've a big camp to keep on an even keel, do you think I came just to see you?'

'No, I don't.'

'Then?'

'Larry said a few words and I told him he was on the wrong track.' Manny was hobbling up the steps, limping back in the direction of the studio. 'I told him that Justin was not arrested or anything.'

'Then thank you for nothing. I strive after a reputation for firmness and you break it down with a few not well chosen words. What were those words? The truth?'

'Yes. I told Larry that Justin was not given over to the law.'

'That was only part of the story. Did you tell the rest?'

Manny flushed. 'Hardly,' she said. 'I didn't want everyone to know that my bridegroom didn't turn up.'

'Did they know he was that?' Huw demanded.

Manny, aggravated, answered deliberately: 'Well, if they did, they've now switched to you.' She went to hobble through the doorway.

The next moment she was swept off her feet and carried right into the studio. When she tried to escape by kicking out at him a voice near her ear advised: 'Remember your toes.'

'Just put me down, Mr Grant!'

'Yes, *Mrs* Grant, if Mrs Grant is what you're trying to tell me about. But it hasn't happened, has it ... not yet.'

'And never will!' Manny, on her feet now, looked furiously at him.

But Huw was not looking back at her, he was staring at the canvas, at the first symbols she had brushed in. After a long moment he said: 'I think love is returning.' He turned quietly and kissed her on her mouth. 'You're a good girl, Emmanuelle.' His voice was soft.

She stood very still after that quiet kiss. He had kissed her before, kissed her in comfort, kissed her in scorn. But this kiss ...

She heard him leave the studio, go down to the kitchen, she heard Jane's and Umberto's voices, Huw's voice.

She put her fingers to her mouth and touched where his lips had touched.

Then determinedly she wiped the kiss off.

CHAPTER SIX

THE next day Huw Grant directed Manny to go into Elkington Town to have his home nursing put to the test.

'I may have left a few germs around,' he said, 'best to be medically checked.'

There was no doctor at Soleil Bay, no anything at all; all supplies, all medical, dental and library help had to come from the hinterland.

It was some thirty kilometres over a rough road into Elkington, but Manny had never minded that, it had meant a day out to her. On this occasion, however, she did not look forward to it; her feet were sore, and she dreaded any application of the brakes.

She felt less enthusiastic again when Jane informed

her that she was coming, too, that she wanted to in-
spect the high school where she would soon enrol.
Manny had had plans for a quick visit to the doctor
and then straight home again, but with Jane there
as well she knew she would have little hope of that.

However, when Jane added that Umberto would
be there to help Manny with the car if she needed
help, Umberto being a skilled driver if still too young
to be licensed, she cheered up.

'Uncle Huw said you'll need someone beside you
because of your injured feet,' Jane told her. 'He's
checked Umberto and says he should do.'

Manny knew she could have no doubts about
Umberto's ability, not after being approved by a Huw
Grant, but she did have doubts about the way the
man seemed to be bringing the two young people
together, especially after her initial directions from
him.

When Huw drove across from his garage then, Umberto beside him, Manny made an excuse to edge
Huw away from the others before she took the
driver's seat.

'You're letting the children get very pally,' she
said directly.

'Isn't that what you recommended?' he returned.

'Not recommended, I merely remarked that first
day that you invited trouble suspecting everyone like
you did.'

'Then I've taken notice of what you said, so what's
wrong?'

'Nothing, if you don't think so.'

He ran his fingers through his hair in exasperation.

'Just make up your mind, Miss Norbert.'

He hesitated, and he grunted: 'Women!

'I have another reason for Umberto's presence,' he went on, 'he's driving the accountant to bursting point. Also the research chemist. Also the engineer. Also every branch I've tried him in. Everyone likes him but no one wants him. Umberto was just not made for work with a pen.'

'What about work with a pin ... a rolling pin?'

'I take your point, but his parents wouldn't. Umberto is here to be tried out as a possible cadet, certainly not anything else. However, he can drive if necessary, for which reason I'm entrusting him with you.'

'That's nice,' Manny came in falsely.

'You and my niece,' Huw tacked on. He nodded Manny back to the waggon, and, the children settled, Manny set off.

It made it easier with Umberto beside her, and they were soon in Elkington Town. At Jane's suggestion they went to the high school first to look around.

'The head is all right,' Umberto assured them after they had walked around the closed school, peered through windows, inspected the playing field. 'If only my mother and father——' He sighed.

'I know,' nodded Jane with fellow feeling, 'my parents are the same. What's the use of all this stuff we get crammed into us when we won't use it?'

Manny thought she had better say something at this juncture, and did so. She made a little speech on the value in every occupation for education.

It was received lukewarmly.

Next Manny called on Elkington's doctor. He said that a fine job had been made, but just in case gave her a prevention shot.

'I think,' fussed Jane, who had come into the surgery with Manny and at once had become the nurse she dreamed about, 'you should have some hot, sweet tea for shock after that. Or' ... an inspiration! ... 'some capuccino.'

'I haven't had a shock, Jane,' Manny pointed out.

'It would be a kind of shock all the same, wouldn't it, Doctor? I suggest going to Umberto's.'

'Umberto's?' This time Manny did feel a slight shock. She had thought that Umberto had come to help her with the car, not to——

'Umberto's people run the White Rose Café, did you know?' They were out of the surgery by now and walking along Elkington's Main Street. Actually it was only a small street and a small town, but after Soleil Bay it became a veritable hub. 'Umberto recommends the toasted sandwiches. He says if we go he'll do them himself.'

When they got to the White Rose, Umberto did do the sandwiches, much to his father's sorrow. Mr Fuccilli came and sat at the table while his son took over, and said sadly to Manny: 'We wish, Mamma and I, to make a gentleman of him, we wish him to put on a suit for work, not a cooking apron.'

'You're wrong, you know,' Jane came in. 'My parents want me to type or something like that, and I want to nurse.'

Manny listened sympathetically to both of them,

yet not very attentively. Her attention instead was on a figure on the other side of the street, a very wide street, as in most country towns. If she hadn't known he was miles away she could have mistaken the back of the man she was looking at as Justin's lithe back, there was the same easy gait, the same rather indolent grace. He was gone almost as soon as she noticed him ... but something remained with her.

Where, she thought suddenly, was Justin now? What was he doing? Did he ever think of her? recall what they both had intended? Did he still intend it one day? ... Did *she*, for all that she had told herself that she had turned a page?

'And now,' Mr Fuccilli was sighing, 'although Umberto is employed by Mr Huw in the company office, he is here instead making sandwiches.'

'They're lovely sandwiches,' Jane praised.

Manny made a few social calls while Jane ate another batch. When her father had died there had been many expressions of sympathy from Elkington, and some senders she wanted to thank in person, having not previously found the time. One of these was the owner of the beach cottage that Hal Norbert had rented for many years, and while the young ones stuffed themselves Manny called round.

She cried a little, accepted a cup of tea that she did not want after the coffee, then said goodbye again, answering the owner's regret that he wouldn't be seeing her so much now that there was a long, paid up lease instead of a weekly rent with a smile and a grateful: 'Thanks to Dad.'

The surprised look in reply was observed by

Manny, but not seriously; her attention was on something else ... some*one* else. A second time she briefly gimpsed the man who could have been Justin, he was entering one of the town's few hotels, and once again his back was turned to her. At what stage, Manny mused to herself, do people not look for likenesses in other people, not imagine they see someone when they know they can't any more?

She went back to the café and announced that it was time to go home.

When they reached Soleil Bay, Larry and some of the men were waiting at the cottage gate for them.

'So he's not with you,' Larry greeted.

'Who?'

'The boss. We haven't seen him all day. We thought he might have decided to go into town as well.'

'He didn't,' Manny informed him. 'He fetched the car over and then watched us off.'

'And hasn't been seen since.' Larry frowned.

'Is that serious?' Manny at this stage was unconcerned.

'It could be, seeing that Grant has always been an on-the-spot boss.' Larry added drily: 'Rather to our dismay.'

Manny skipped that, and asked: 'Where have you looked for him?'

'Everywhere we can think. Along the beach, round the headland, in the bush. It all started when one of the engineers had an enquiry but no one to enquire from.'

'You searched the office section?'

'Each room, even inside the filing cabinet.' But Larry was not laughing as he said it.

'Every part of the mining?' Manny asked.

'Every sand grain of it.'

'What about the sand buggy, he might have taken that.'

'It's still here. No, wherever he's gone, he's gone on foot.'

'He could have been testing,' said Manny. There was always testing going on for new rutile evidence.

'We thought that, and the rest of the men are out now searching. He could have fallen somewhere, you see. Worse still, there could have been a sand-slide.'

Manny nodded grimly now. If that had happened they had trouble, she thought.

Wisely she did not offer to search as well, her feet would have been an encumbrance, not a help. But she nodded when Jane and Umberto asked permission to join the party.

An hour went by, and Manny, keeping the kettle boiling in case the men got back and tea was needed, began to worry. It made it so much harder when night was approaching, she thought, and, looking out on a first darkling, dusk was not far off.

She went out to the verandah, back to the kitchen, she boiled up again.

She could not have said what made her go to the studio, she was in no mood for painting, or even observing what she had done. But something must have urged her, and the moment she walked in she gave a little cry.

Huw lay on the floor and an easel lay on top of him. It still rested on his head. There was blood on his temple, and he must have been there for some time, because the blood was beginning to congeal.

She knelt down at once to make sure that his neck was not turned unnaturally, his arms not trapped and crushed under him, but everything was normal, there was only that wound.

She had his head in her lap now, knowing, since nothing else seemed amiss, that he must be concussed.

'Huw,' she said, 'Huw, wake up!' She wondered how long he had been like this.

She tried to take his pulse, but could not feel it. In desperation she put her lips to his mouth, but before she could start anything he said clearly: 'If that's intended for mouth-to-mouth resuscitation, Emmanuelle, you close the nostrils first. But on the other hand if it's intended for something else, please go ahead and kiss.'

He had opened his eyes, those sharp silver eyes of his, and was looking up at her. He gave a little grin.

'You fraud!' Manny cried. 'You pretended you were——'

'No, not at all, I *was* knocked out. After you left I came in here to have another look at the work ... don't you ever lock up? ... and that wretched easel clocked me. I don't know how long I was out, but I'm all right now, except for an egg on my head, I should think. But' ... still lying on the floor ... 'do go ahead.'

'I'll do no such thing! The men are out looking for you, what they'll say when they know you've been here all the time I can't imagine.'

'I can. They'll grin to each other: "The *Grants* are at it again."'

'At least you could have called out to them before they left to look for you,' ignored Manny.

'I could not, I've only this moment become unconcussed. Please give me a hand up.' He wanted to rise and he waited for her help.

When she hesitated he said: 'You can kiss me standing as well as prone if that's what's worrying you.'

'Oh, get up!' Manny took his hand and hauled.

He followed her out to the kitchen and stood watching her as she did unnecessary things to kettle and cups, unnecessary because when the men returned there would be no call now for succour, they could go back to their mess.

'How did Elkington go?' Huw asked casually, watching Manny from a perch on the kitchen table now.

'Quite well. We did the school first, then the doctor, as ordered by you. Then we had coffee at the White Rose, as suggested by Jane. Umberto made it, also the sandwiches, and very nice they were, too. His parents own the café, and, as you said, are not happy about their son.'

Huw nodded wryly. 'Poor Umberto. What else?'

'I called in on the owner of Dad's ... I mean my house, a Mr Leicester. Harry.'

'Yes, I know.'

'Do you?' She looked at him, a little surprised.

'... Well, heard of him. Why did you go there?'

'To thank him for his kindness after Father's death.' Manny paused. 'Then we came home.'

Huw was silent for a few moments. 'Anything else?' he asked presently.

'Nothing else.' Manny looked at him wonderingly. 'Why?'

He looked back at her, looked searchingly, narrowly, not speaking.

Manny felt herself flushing and was annoyed because she could not stop it. There had been nothing, but her pink cheeks said otherwise, she knew. That illusion of Justin had been only that, illusion. But suddenly, as in town, she was asking questions of herself. If it had not been her imagination, if the man actually had been Justin, Justin whom she had gone to Sydney to marry, would she have run after him? Would she have——

'I don't know.' She was unaware that she said it aloud, but Huw picked her up.

'You don't know what? My dear Manny, I suspect you of not answering me fully just now. Are you sure nothing else happened in town?'

'Why don't you go in and see for yourself?'

'Be assured if I doubt you enough I'll do just that.'

'I am assured,' she snapped. 'Here are the searchers to be assured about you. Rather an anticlimax to find you safe and sound, I think.'

'Also a disappointment?' he suggested drily.

'Why don't you ask them?' Manny turned away.

The two young people were with the volunteers. One of the men's: 'So you're all right, boss' was lost in Jane's girlish:

'Oh, Uncle Huw, you're not dead after all! What happened? Aren't we having a lot of catastrophes lately? Did you fall over? Did Manny resuscitate you—you have a red splodge across your mouth.'

Huw said: 'Yes, Jane, from a kiss.' He added for all of them: 'A kiss of life.'

'I've never seen that done, do you think you and Manny could——'

'No, I certainly don't think.' Huw turned to the men. 'I was fixing the easel for Miss Norbert and it turned and fixed me. Some time later Miss Norbert did what she thought fit, she revived me by a kiss of life. I'm quite recovered now, no need to collect for a wreath of roses.'

Larry said in a dry voice: 'The flowers would have been forget-me-nots, sir.'

'Thanks,' Huw said evenly. 'It's nice to be remembered.'

'Nice of you always to remember us,' responded Larry. 'No doubt Welsh thought that.'

There was a sudden silence. Standing near the door, Manny listened but did not look.

'Want to go further with that?' Huw invited.

'No,' Larry answered.

'All right, then. Cook must be wondering how he can keep things hot any longer. We'd better get across.'

There was no answer, but Manny heard the party leave. Huw must have left with them, taking Umberto with him, for only Jane came into the house.

Because Jane had devoured too many toasted sandwiches she was not ready for supper. She asked

Manny if she was hungry and when Manny said she was not she suggested waiting until they were.

She followed Manny to the studio and perched on a stool while Manny examined the mural.

Jane was not interested in painting, but she was interested in the easel that had concussed Huw.

'Yes,' she said, trying to be professional, 'Uncle Huw could have been fatally injured but for your mouth-to-mouth. I really must learn it from you. Oh, Manny, talking of learning only makes me think again of my waste of valuable years going back to school.'

'You're not old enough for nursing yet, Jane.'

'For an aide I'm old enough.'

'Barely, and in the time left until you are you should absorb all the knowledge you can.'

'Latin!' scoffed Jane.

'It comes into everything,' Manny reminded her, 'especially, I would say, in medical matters.'

'I can do without it, and so, he says, can Umberto. How could Latin help a quiche lorraine?'

'*Mensa*, a table,' suggested Manny, wondering whether to move the Teetering Stone an inch.

'They work on benches, not tables. Oh, Manny, it is awful, and you must agree.'

'I don't agree. Schools are different now, you could even do the home science course—no Latin there.'

'But it still would be school.'

'School for Umberto, too, remember; he's three months younger than you are.'

'Manny, do you know what?' Jane asked in

pleased surprise. 'I'd completely forgotten about Umberto being younger.'

'Of course,' Manny said abstractedly, she considered the balance of the first panel of the mural was right at last.

Not till later did she recall Jane's statement ... and find an inbalance. 'I'd completely forgotten about Umberto being younger,' Jane had said.

Manny gave that some thought.

CHAPTER SEVEN

A WEEK followed without any of Jane's 'catastrophes', and by then the school vacation was over, the new term beginning, and tomorrow Jane would enrol at Elkington High. Manny thought about this as she covered the mural for the night and obeyed Jane's call for supper. Jane, very proud of her culinary skill, very fetching in a pink apron, drooped pathetically when Manny was misguided enough to bring the subject up. She even pushed her own plate aside, unheard-of from Jane who had a huge, growing girl appetite, but that, Manny suspected, could have been from too much sampling during the cooking.

'I'm sorry, Jane,' Manny said penitently, 'I shouldn't have spoiled your last night. You look so nice, too.'

'I know I do, Manny. Aprons suit me. Men see me

and think I would be nice to have in their kitchen. But they won't think that tomorrow. You see, not having an Elkington tunic yet, I asked Uncle Huw if I could wear my own gear, and he said No, wear your St Helen's until you buy your new outfit. Manny, St Helen's is awful—All navy serge and pleats! It's never been altered since the school was established.'

'Lots of former day fashions are coming back,' Manny assured her.

'St Helen's never left.'

'Well, Elkington High might be better.'

'Yes.' Jane brightened slightly. 'On the other hand,' she said soon after, gloomy again, 'I have to depart from this house tomorrow, and when the men see me——'

'We'll try to see that they don't. I'm to drive you to the crossroads to pick up the school bus. If you get in the car before we go through the gates and sit right down——'

'I have to come home, too, remember.'

'Then we'll repeat the performance,' Manny cheered.

Jane not very hopefully agreed.

The next day Jane did what Manny had proposed, but halfway down the narrow lane that led to the road to Elkington she found she had left behind her a necessary report from her old school.

'Uncle Huw said that when he rang the Elkington Head he was told to remind me to bring it,' Jane wailed. 'Now I'll have to run back and the men will see me.'

'No one was about when we came out, Jane—and

anyhow, I'll go.' Manny got out of the car and returned to the house.

She searched everywhere for the report but could not find it. Glancing up at the clock, she saw that if she didn't leave at once they would not be in time for the school bus.

She started back to the car, but Jane met her halfway.

'It was in my bag all the time.' She held the bag up. 'I'm sorry, Manny—— Oh, Manny!' She nodded self-consciously in the direction of the sand-mining. Jane had not restricted her interest only to Umberto, she had sorted out a few of the others she considered not too antiquated and rather dishy, and now this selection sat on the fence watching her with unconcealed delight. Manny could understand their amusement. Last week they had looked sidewise at a young charmer replete with dangling ear-rings, piled-up hair, blue eyeshadow, luscious lips, and now they saw flat college shoes, pleated serge, a pale mouth, a high-necked school shirt. Also, horror of horrors, a panama hat. No wonder they applauded!

One of them had found a bell, probably the cook's bell, and he rang it impudently. 'School's in!' he called.

Red with mortification, Jane got into the car again and Manny drove as fast as she could to the cross-roads.

They just made it, the bus came lumbering along within a minute. Manny watched Jane off, knowing that in this young company Jane would have no more trouble, that in a country school bus not knowing everyone can last only a few seconds. She should know, Manny thought, she had been a commuting pupil herself. She waited till the bus resumed its way, then came back to the car and drove home again.

Even though Jane had taken over the household chores, there was now much more time for work, Manny soon found. Always Jane had had something to say, or she would bring in a dish for Manny to sample, or hold a conference as to what she should concoct for their next meal, so that in the end there had been more hours spent on chatter than painting. But now Manny found she could really apply herself, assured that Jane was safe and accounted for, no longer half listening for a door to open, then shut again while she wondered uneasily should she follow up to see what Jane was doing, since that, as well as the mural commission, was what she was here for.

She uncovered the mural and worked hard for several hours.

In her deep absorption she did not hear Huw come in, silently pull out an old stool, then sit down and watch her. It was only when she stood back to survey what she had done that she stepped on something that immediately reacted with a pained grunt. She turned in alarm and found Huw rubbing his ankle.

'Serves you right!' She looked at him indignantly. 'If I'd known you'd crept in to spy on me——'

'I did not creep and I was not spying,' he told her.

'Then——'

'I had a very relaxing hour seeing you work.'

Manny brushed aside his relaxation and instead shuddered at being observed and not knowing.

'I could have done anything,' she objected.

'Like?'

'A dozen things. Like making myself more comfortable, for instance. If I get hot painting sometimes I throw off.'

'Throw off?'

'Clothes,' she mumbled, sorry she had started. 'Also when a line won't go as I want it to go, I say things. I wipe my brush—— well, anywhere.'

'That last you've done already, you have a smudge of vermilion on your nose.' Huw reached for his handkerchief and began rubbing her. Manny tried to edge off, but each time she stepped back, he stepped forward with her, still rubbing. Nonetheless she still retreated until a wall halted her. Perforce he had to stop, too, only some several inches away.

'You've painted yourself into a corner,' he quipped, but Manny could not raise a quip back. Seen as close as only a breath away as he was now, his silver eyes seemed to dominate his face, and dominate her. She tried to tilt her head away to escape that encompassing silver, but the wall prevented her and instead sent her head tilting towards him again. He caught it with his hands and held it firmly, then, his hold still firm, lifted up her face to his and kissed her.

This time Manny did escape, she ducked under his arm, exclaiming furiously: 'You're always doing that!'

'Used you say that to Welsh? Also as a matter of interest, I've done it twice.'

'Three times.'

'So you count!' he exclaimed with apparent delight.

'What did you come over for?' Manny demanded. 'I mean, besides spying on me?'

'To find out how Jane got away.'

'In great embarrassment,' she told him. 'Some of your younger men were out and poor Jane looked very much a schoolgirl.'

He laughed.

'A pity,' he said, 'that Umberto had stopped working for us, because he too might have had second thoughts.' He stepped back to the work she had done and examined it silently for several minutes.

'Well?' Manny asked at last.

'Yes,' he replied.

'Yes?'

'It's very good, Emmanuelle.' He turned and smiled at her, and, in spite of herself, Manny felt a glow. She said, a little mollified:

'I'll do a little more before lunch. If you want to stop and watch that's all right by me.'

'Thank you, but as I've done my watching, as you've had your praise, if we stop together any longer it will be for more than that.' He looked meaningly at her.

'I don't follow you.' Manny could feel the treacherous pink rising in her cheeks.

'No?' Huw said in laughter, and while she fumbled angrily for words to retort, he left.

Manny worked hotly for a while, but the spirit had forsaken her, she was no longer in the mood.

Presently she put down her brush and went outside to make lunch. After the meal she walked for a while, pausing often to sketch something that she might introduce into the first mural panel, her interpretation of Soleil Bay as it had been in the beginning. When she got back to the cottage she saw it was time to drive to the crossroads to pick up Jane from school.

From Manny's own experience in school buses the atmosphere coming home was always much more cheerful than going. But when Jane alighted she was certainly no figure of joy.

'What went wrong, Jane?' Manny asked anxiously as the bus gained speed once more. 'Couldn't you make friends?'

'Oh, that was easy enough, though all the travelling kids are junior to me, no contemptuous ones at all.'

'Contemporary,' corrected Manny. 'Then what went wrong?'

'The uniform, for one thing. Guess what Elkington High uniform is? Serge and pleats again! In fact the Head said this St Helen's one would do. But the worst part was the course that I'm to take. I explained very clearly to Mr Ferris how I wouldn't be needing the usual subjects so would concentrate on ones that would really benefit me, and he refused even to consider it. The moment we get home I'm going across to Uncle Huw and insist he rings up the Head at once.'

'Yes, dear,' said Manny meekly, for it was the only reply she could think of. She knew that Huw would not ring, and she did not blame him, but she still felt sorry for Jane.

She tried to divert her by telling her how she had missed her, how long the day had seemed without her, and what did she think they should have for supper? Jane responded, but she still retained her feeling of being badly done by, and the moment they reached the house she marched across to the mining, not even bothering to change out of her serge pleats.

She was back in an incredibly short time.

'Was your uncle out?' Manny asked.

'No, but I was, in two seconds. Oh, Manny, Uncle Huw is so unfair! Why do I have to know algebra when I'll be nursing sick people? Umberto's the same. He's in the science class learning about molecules when he should be absorbing Béchamel sauce.'

'But, Jane, a background of learning is always a valuable thing,' Manny assured her.

'It's a waste of time, and I haven't so much of that. I'm sixteen.'

'Fifteen and a half, Jane. Now about supper . . .'

But Manny cooked it that night . . . also the nights after. A week of nights. Jane seemed to have lost interest. On the other hand, Manny thought, the girl did appear . . . well, more or less . . . to be settling somewhat. There was no more talk of wasted years, and Jane went off each morning no longer bemoaning serge pleats.

Then——

School was well into its second week when Manny pulled up the car at the crossroads and waited for the bus to drop Jane. She had no misgivings any longer; Jane, though much quieter than the earlier Jane, had apparently fallen into the accepted pattern.

Manny looked around her as she waited for the rumble of the rather antiquated transport. The crossroads was the junction to several small coastal villages, and as pretty as a picture. Manny took out her pad, determined to put the crossroads into her picture.

The next moment she looked up in surprise: the bus, not heard in her absorption, had lumbered past and was now well down the road. Foolishly Manny looked round for Jane, mentally reminding herself to scold the girl for jumping out before the bus stopped. But had the bus stopped? She had heard nothing. If it had, and Jane had alighted, where was she now?

She got out and went round the back of the car. Perhaps Jane, seeing her absorption, had decided to play a prank. But no Jane jumped out. Manny looked around, but there were only empty paddocks, nowhere for anyone to hide. She called: 'Jane!' then felt silly when only a crow called back.

She got into the car and began following the now no longer visible bus. After eight minutes, because it only lumbered, and because it had to stop at farm gates to disgorge children, she caught up. She tooted, then when the bus came to a shuddering halt hopped out of her car and went and enquired for Jane.

The driver gave her a pained look. Every day he transported a busload of juniors, how was he to know which was Jane? He turned to his passengers. Yes, they all knew Jane. She was the new one. She got in and out at the crossroads, only today she hadn't been there to get out, so the bus had not stopped. You had to ring the bell when you got out, seventeen voices shouted eagerly. But why Jane hadn't got out they could not tell Manny. Probably she had been given detention for something. Or she might be rehearsing for the school play. Or going to a meeting. Or——

'But she knows she has to catch the bus to get home,' Manny said worriedly.

'Then she missed it,' they advised.

The driver, anxious to get on, said that undoubtedly Jane would come out of some car, so not to worry. Before Manny could worry in front of him, he started off.

Manny drove back to the crossroads. If Jane wangled a lift out she would get off here, so she would wait for her. She parked the car in the usual position and did so.

No cars came, which was not surprising, for the road, except at week-ends, or when the mining lorries came in from Soleil with their spoil, was always deserted.

After an hour Manny decided to go back to the bay. Perhaps Jane had got her lift in the time that she had spent chasing the bus, had even got a lift right out. She started the engine and stepped hard on the accelerator.

Even when she reached the cottage and Jane was not there, Manny, though concerned, did nothing. Possibly Jane had come home, found no one around, so gone for a walk. There was only one place to walk, it was down to the beach.

Manny took the track beside the mining. There

was no one in sight, no one on the headland. Had
Jane disobeyed the cardinal rule and gone into the
works?

Or perhaps she had gone swimming, though to
date she had not evinced much interest in that direction, only in sitting on the beach in a bikini. But if
she had ... Really troubled now, Manny looked to
the sea and the sea looked implacably back.

She returned to the house. She waited another
hour. At any moment Jane, free of detention or
whatever it was that had kept her, would jump out
of some returning car and amble into the house.
Manny kept reassuring herself of that. But what if no
car had been returning and Jane had set out to walk?
It was a long, long walk ... miles ... and Jane was
not a walker. All the same Manny walked herself, she
walked down the narrow track that led to the Elkington road. If nothing else it was action.

There was very little room, if you met a car you
had to plunge into the bush. Manny heard a car coming and duly plunged ... but once there she lay low.
For a quick look had told her that Jane was not in
the car ... *but that Huw Grant was.* She waited in
the scrub until the car disappeared from sight, then
she decided to return to the house.

She looked around carefully before she did so,
then when she saw no one around she re-entered the
cottage the back way.

The place lay in silence. Manny stood at the
kitchen window willing the sun, that seemed to be
hurrying to the west much sooner than it should, to
delay a while. It was bad enough mislaying Jane in

daylight, but to have her still absent at night ...

But in spite of Manny's wishing, the inevitable shadows began creeping into the room. Manny knew she could delay no longer, she would simply have to cross to the works and report to Huw.

But before she did so she could ring the school. There might be a simple explanation. Why hadn't she thought of that before?

She went into the hall, quite dark now, and took up the phone.

She had dialled the school number and was waiting for a response when she became aware that Huw Grant was standing at the other end of the hall watching her.

'Where have you been?' he demanded irritably. 'I've been waiting for you to get back.'

She could have answered that she had been standing at the kitchen window looking for his niece, but she said equally irritably: 'Back from where?'

'Back from the track. You dived into the scrub when you saw me coming—oh, yes, I saw you. What was it? Guilty conscience? Or didn't you want my company?'

Manny only replied: 'Why are you here?'

'To know why you take such pains to avoid me.'

'You come into my house uninvited for that?'

What he would have answered, Manny was not to know, though she could see by his angry eyes that words were certainly there, for at that moment there was a voice on the wire, and to her dismay she realised that she was still standing dangling the phone, that she had not cut off.

'Elkington High.' The principal's voice, very clear, loud enough to be heard by Huw as well as Manny, came booming through. 'What is it, please?'

'Sorry, wrong number.' Manny put down the phone.

CHAPTER EIGHT

'WASN'T that the school?' Huw Grant had crossed to Manny's side and he was looking down at the phone and at her.

'Evidently you heard for yourself!' Manny snapped in reply. Her nerves felt taut.

'I *thought* the voice said Elkington High,' Huw persisted. 'Did it?'

'... Yes.'

'Then why did you put the phone down? Why were you rung from the school?'

'I—I don't know.'

'No, you don't know because you killed the call. You said wrong number. Why did you do that?'

There was no answer.

'... Or' ... probingly now from Huw ... 'had you rung in to Elkington and not the school out to Soleil?'

'Oh, for heaven's sake!' Now Manny's nerves were near snapping, but Huw ignored her protest.

'There's something going on, and I know it will be to do with Jane. What is it this time? She doesn't like her gym dress? She doesn't care about panama hats? Lace-up shoes? The stripe in her tie? It has to be something of the sort, for I've already exhausted her dissatisfaction with the curriculum. One entire hour I had over the phone with Ferris, who incidentally seems a very nice fellow, and——' Huw stopped abruptly, obviously recalling that he had not yet settled whether Manny had rung the school or the school rung her.

Seeing his intending look, Manny insisted quickly: 'It was just a wrong number.'

'And you're just a bad liar. Answer me, Emmanuelle, did you ring them or did they ring you?' As she did not answer he took an intentional step closer and insisted: 'Well?'

'I rang them,' she said wearily.

'Then you should have let me do that.' Now his tone was much milder, even gentle. 'Although I've employed you to keep an eye on Jane I don't want you harassed with all her teenage problems.'

'If that was all——' It came out spontaneously, and Manny could have bitten out her tongue.

'If that was all! What are you talking about? Is something wrong? Something more than teenage problems? *Tell* me, Manny.'

'Yes, I will,' Manny said desperately, knowing she could hold out no longer. 'I rang the high school to ask them—to ask them——'

'Go on.'

'Why Jane wasn't home yet. Then when I saw you here I got frightened, so I said what I did.'

'Wrong number,' he nodded. Then the impact of what she had just told him reached him. 'Not home yet?' he echoed. 'But it's dusk. It's near night!'

'She wasn't on the bus this afternoon,' Manny explained. 'I spoke to the driver and to the children, and learned that she hadn't travelled with them from Elkington. I came back here, thinking she might have got a lift home. When she wasn't in the house I went down to the beach.' Manny shivered in memory. 'Then I decided that, being Jane, she might even attempt to walk home, so——'

'So you started to walk yourself, met me coming down the track, hid until I'd gone by, then came back again.'

'Yes. After that I stood watching from the kitchen window, because I knew that the back way was the way she would probably come.' Manny added forlornly: 'If she came.'

'When, not if,' Huw said determinedly. 'My God, Manny, why didn't you tell me all this before?'

'I was afraid.'

'Afraid for Jane or yourself?'

'I suppose for both of us,' she admitted.

'You're saying you're afraid of me?'

Manny lowered her glance, and it was sufficient reply.

'Am I such a tyrant, then?' he asked.

'I don't know,' was all Manny could think to answer.

'I was waiting in the studio for you,' Huw said after a long pause. He looked tired all of a sudden, tired, older, and somehow defeated. 'Yes, I suppose you could say a waiting tyrant.' He gave a little hunch of his shoulders. He was silent for a few moments, then he stirred himself.

'I'll ring Elkington now, hear the worst.'

'Why do you always expect the worst with Jane?'
she asked crossly.

'Because I think of Judy,' he said at once.

'Judy, the rash one.'

He gave her a quick, closing kind of look, then
turned and picked up the phone.

This time the Head could not have been far away,
for a response came at once. In the same close position now as Huw had been before when she had held
the phone, Manny heard Mr Ferris boom: 'Elkington High, what is it, please?'

Then she heard Huw speak.

It was Grant from Soleil Bay, he said, and he was
enquiring about his niece Jane. Had she been
kept——

'Oh, yes, Mr Grant,' broke in Mr Ferris quite
audibly. 'When she didn't come to classes today we
gathered it would be some indisposition. These growing years, Grant, are not always easy for an ado-
lescent.'

'She didn't come to school!' Huw's voice rose. 'But
she took the school bus. At least I think——' Huw
turned to Manny, and Manny nodded. 'Yes,' he said
into the phone, but more quietly, 'she took the bus.'

'Then she didn't come here.' Now Mr Ferris's
voice had sharpened. 'Have you contacted any of her
fellow travellers? They should know whether Jane
arrived at the school when they did.'

Manny put out her hand, and at a nod from Huw
took the receiver from him.

'This is Manny Norbert, Mr Ferris, and the children would be of no use because all the travellers on

Jane's bus are in lower grades, or so she told me, and you know what that means when you're young, it comprises practically another world. At the most they would only know her name.'

There was silence at the other end. Then Mr Ferris spoke again.

'We naturally thought she was ill, a common occurrence, as I said. This means Jane has been absent all day.'

'Yes,' Huw called. He was sharing the phone with Manny now.

'I'll begin telephoning Jane's classmates,' said Mr Ferris, 'some of them might know.'

'I don't think so,' Manny negated. 'She hasn't been there long enough to really get to know anyone, in fact she hasn't spoken of anyone, except Umberto, and she knew him previously from his working out here.'

'Umberto Fuccilli.' Mr Ferris's voice came sharply again. 'But Umberto, too, was away today. I know because I myself take one of his subjects, and I marked him down as not having attended. Will you stand by, please, and I'll ring back.' He put the phone down.

Manny, abstracted, still stood with their own receiver tight in her hand, and Huw took it from her and replaced it. 'Otherwise,' he pointed out, 'we won't hear any ring.'

His voice was flat.

It was ten minutes before the telephone pealed and in all that time neither of them moved or spoke. Huw picked the phone up.

'Yes.—Yes, Mr Ferris.—I see.—No, sir, I'll take up from there.—Yes, of course I'll let you know.— Thank you, I would appreciate that. The fewer people told at this juncture—— Yes, sir.'

Now he put the receiver back.

'Ferris has been in touch with the Fuccilis,' he said, 'and Umberto, too, has not come home. He left for school this morning, as Jane did, but he never arrived either, and he too is now unaccounted for. It could be a coincidence, but in the circumstances that seems unlikely, so we now have to face this, Manny: in all probability those two kids, Jane and Umberto, have gone off together. But why? Where? Manny, where are we now?'

The stunned look on Huw's face shocked Manny. She had not thought that this obviously self-disciplined man could react so deeply. But of course, his was the sole responsibility of Jane during her parents' absence. Yet even allowing for this onerous job, Huw Grant's distress still disturbed her. As unemotionally as she could she said: 'There could be several explanations, I expect.'

He looked at her quite starkly. 'Give me one.'

She tried, but failed. The only real reason she knew she had to offer was the children's mutual dissatisfaction at what life appeared to be handing out to them, their instinctive drawing together because of that, but she could not say so to this concerned man. For without his spelling it out she knew intrinsically what he was thinking. He was anticipating that Jane and Umberto ... that they ...

'They're children,' she said impulsively.

'So was——' But he stopped himself. 'Where?' he asked instead. '*Where*, Manny? Where do two fed-up teenagers go?'

'Ordinarily I would say to the town coffee shop to mull things over, but Umberto's parents own the only coffee shop, so that's out.'

'But even so would they mull all day,' Huw argued, 'even' ... looking down the darkling passage ... 'into the night? For it's night now. If we don't find them it's going to be tomorrow. Manny, think. Manny, help me!'

Manny nodded, suddenly beyond speech.

Their impulse at first was to get out a car, begin action, start something. But Manny took hold of the situation. If she didn't, she was thinking, then certainly, from his distraught look, Huw couldn't. He was grey in spite of his deep tan, and he kept running his hand through his hair.

'We'll eat something first,' she ordered crisply, 'while I'm fixing it, you tidy yourself up. You're disorderly, and you don't know where you'll be called to go tonight.'

'I hardly think so. The youngsters wouldn't have enough money for the Ritz. But I know what you mean, and I will tidy up.' Huw went a few steps, then he turned. 'Thank you, Emmanuelle.'

Manny made a pot of tea and quickly cut some sandwiches. By the time Huw emerged from the bathroom duly brushed and combed the meal was on the table. Manny filled two mugs, then nodded to a chair. Neither of them spoke until some of the sandwiches were consumed and second cups started.

'Now?' Huw asked Manny.

'Yes,' said Manny.

'Then what do we do?' he began. 'Where do we start?'

'We start looking, naturally,' Manny answered, 'but, as you just said, where?' She pushed aside her cup and put her elbows on the table. 'The Fuccilis?' she began.

'The Headmaster is taking them over, so at least we're spared their tears and fears. No, think of somewhere else.'

'It can't be Soleil Bay, there's only this cottage and your mining.'

'Caves,' he reminded her, his voice frayed. Manny knew what he was implying, and even though she shrank from the implication she could not discard it. At nearly sixteen the modern child was no longer a child in body. She gave an instinctive glance through the window, suddenly hating the moon for being so round and gold tonight, the stars so silver. Somewhere those two could be watching the same moon and stars, dreaming youth's long, long dreams ... then quietly drifting into something beyond dreaming.

'No,' Manny said firmly.

'Elkington Town,' suggested Huw. 'Would they be there?'

'Have they any transport?' Manny asked.

'Yes, when he rang back the Head told me that the Fuccilis had reported that Umberto had taken the car.'

'Then they wouldn't be at Elkington, it's too public, too familiar, yet I hardly think they could be far out of it. Petrol is too dear for long journeys these days, and I don't believe that Umberto would have much ready cash, he has very frugal parents. As for Jane, you've kept her down to the bone.'

'Deliberately,' said Huw.

They sat silent for a while, then Huw broke the thoughtful quiet.

'You're only five years away,' he said puzzlingly.

'Five years away?' she queried.

'From sixteen. You can't have forgotten how sixteen was. Travel back, Manny, what were your thoughts then?'

'I don't know if I did think very much, I was never brainy.'

'You painted,' he pointed out.

'Only in Dad's shadow, I can't remember having any real ambition in that direction.'

'But you had thoughts of something, you must have had. What were they? You wanted to travel? Go on the stage? Become a diplomat?'

'I suppose I saw myself in a nurse's heroic red cape—most girls do. Also I expect I dreamed of falling in love. Oh, dear!' Manny gave a wry look.

'Both of which would be very applicable to Jane,' Huw agreed. 'Especially' ... his voice sharpened ... 'the falling in love?'

'Huw, you can't think——'

'Of course I think. I have to. Look, Manny, I'm not wasting any more time.' He got up.

Manny got up, too. 'Where are we going?'

'You'll come, too?'

'Of course. But where?'

'Heaven knows,' was all Huw said.

He went across to the project and was back again in the waggon in minutes. He put his foot down on the accelerator even before they reached the twisting lane to Elkington road, and that, Manny could have told him, was something one could not do. At the second snake bend the wheels left the narrow track and the car plunged into the bordering bush. It did not go far, the coarse underbrush stopped it. There was a thud, a thump, and then the waggon shuddered, then stopped dead.

'Damn!' muttered Huw. On a second thought he asked: 'Are you all right?'

'Yes, I am, but I think your waggon isn't.'

'I know it isn't.' He was trying to spark the engine, but to no avail. Presently he sighed: 'I'll have to go back and raise some of the men.'

'To move it back to the track?'

'No, to move it further in, I think the waggon will need repairs, and we haven't time for that. I'll have to ask them to loan me one of their cars. Anyway, we'll have the path cleared whatever else we do. Because we're still searching, Manny, even if every wheel falls off every vehicle we're not giving up. Those two have to be found tonight.'

'Yes, Huw,' said Manny.

She remained in the car while he ran back to the rutile. She tried the waggon lights to see if they were still operable, because when the men came they would need all the illumination they could get.

Although the lights had gone out when the car

had left the track, now for some reason they worked again, Manny found. She looked along the beam of light the switch of a button had produced, then gasped.

Walking along the track, hand in hand, two figures came out of the dark.

Jane. Umberto.

CHAPTER NINE

MANNY was out of the waggon in a flash and running towards Jane and Umberto. Her impulse was to keep running, to call out in relief, but with difficulty she curbed herself, slowed down to a walk, then said as casually as she could: 'I'm glad you two are back. Now I can start supper. I'm starved!'

'Oh, M-Manny,' Jane faltered, and came right up to her.

A little sheepishly Umberto came close behind.

'We'll go to the house,' Manny told the pair a little thickly, for she was all choked up. She led the way back to the cottage. As they passed through the gate a posse of men emerged from the works opposite, and nodding the children inside Manny hurried across to Huw, who led the gang, and said quietly: 'They're back. I'm going to make them something hot.'

'*Afterwards*,' he ordered peremptorily.

'*Afterwards?* Oh, you mean after you've dealt with this ditching waggon?'

'After I've said a few pertinent words to that pair and they've said a few pertinent words back to me.'

'But they could be hungry.'

'Good,' he replied. He turned to the waiting men. 'You'll find the waggon about halfway along the track.'

'Also off the track.' It was Larry's voice, deliberately low-pitched but at the same time deliberately clear.

'That's right.' Huw's own voice was cool. He got into step beside Manny and they walked to the cottage.

'That fellow is trying to get under my skin,' he said.

'Larry wouldn't mean it,' she insisted.

'He certainly means it, he never lets an opportunity go by. He's a good worker but a better agitator.'

'He doesn't see it as agitating.'

'Not missing a chance to put me down? The waggon, for instance. He doesn't take it as my misfortune, he takes it as his advantage. He's now implying that I was driving badly.'

'You were,' said Manny. 'The track can't accept speed. But Larry still doesn't mean it, not really. My father always called him an "agin" type, but he has a good heart.'

'Also a strange idea of goodness. His support of Welsh, for instance.'

'Larry will only tolerate fair play.'

'Correction, he will only tolerate those who are not bosses. I've had experience with Larrys before. But I can handle them.'

'Like you handle everyone?' Manny, incensed because she was fond of her old friend, said sharply. 'Your niece, Mr Grant? How well have you handled her?'

'Shall we find out?' Huw held open the gate.

'We'll find out after the children eat,' Manny tried again.

'Before they eat,' he precluded. 'Waiting a little longer won't starve them—indeed, with everything brought out and aired, appetites should be improved. Will you lead the way? If I appear first they might make a guilty dash for it.'

'You're always anticipating trouble, you're always suspicious,' she said crossly.

'Always,' he nodded calmly. He followed Manny down the hall.

Jane and Umberto sat upright on two chairs; they looked pale and tired, and Manny's heart went out to them. How could Huw Grant not be moved, too? she thought indignantly. She gave him a covert look but could find nothing, neither censure nor concern. The man must be steel. She saw how his eyes had narrowed.

'Emmanuelle seems to think you're famished,' he began. 'However, I would think a few hamburgers on the way have seen to that.'

They both shook their heads.

'We needed every cent for petrol,' Jane proffered, 'it's a long way to Pennington.'

'Pennington?' he queried.

'There are two hospitals there, Uncle Huw.' Jane looked promptingly at Umberto.

'There are five hotels, two of them three-star,' Umberto said. 'There are several superior restaurants.'

'I take it by that that you two were intending to join the working world,' Huw deduced.

'Yes,' they said in unison, 'only——'

'Only?'

They looked wretchedly at each other and were silent.

To Manny's surprise Huw did not pursue the subject.

'Where did you intend living during your working days?' he asked instead. 'Pennington is too far away for daily commuting from Soleil or Elkington.' He spoke drily.

'We thought we would live-in,' said Jane.

Huw looked up sharply at that. 'Live where?' he demanded.

'Live in, Uncle Huw,' explained Jane, 'live-in with a hyphen between the live and the in. I was going to live-in at the hospital and Umberto at the hotel. Only——'

There was no 'Only?' from Huw this time, and a few silent moments went by.

'We had our school lunches,' Umberto proffered. 'We ate those.'

'I'm going to cook something.' Manny got up.

Huw snapped: 'Sit down!' He turned to the children again. 'I want the whole bit. Now. Either of you will do.'

Jane began first. 'I caught the school bus as usual, but I didn't go to school.'

'Purposely or on the spur of the moment?'

'Purposely.'

'I didn't go to school purposely, either,' Umberto said.

'You'd both schemed this?'

'Yes.'

'Why? Fed-up with home? Tired of restraint? Kicking over the traces? Out for a lark?' Casually Huw added: '... Love?'

The two young people looked back at him in complete surprise. 'No, school,' they said together.

'I wanted to be doing nursing things, not what I was doing,' Jane said.

'I wanted sauces, not science,' Umberto answered.

'And that was all?'

'Yes.' Again they spoke in surprise together.

There was a longer silence now in the room. It seemed to go on and on. Manny had a mad impression that had she looked at Huw she would have found hidden laughter somewhere.

'And now, seeing you're back again, you no longer want these things?' Huw enquired.

'No.'

'Why? What gave you a change of heart?'

This time Umberto answered alone. 'It was a change of mind, really, sir. I think our hearts are still the other way. But we talked it over together after——'

'Yes,' broke in Jane, 'after——'

'After what?' Huw's silver eyes had narrowed again.

To Manny's dismay both the children looked down guiltily.

'It was this way, Uncle Huw,' Jane blurted. 'The

hospital *did* want aides, and *did* agree to take me. That is' ... a falter ... 'if I could pass a basic test.' A shamed pause. 'I failed.'

Umberto took up the story. 'I could have got in at a hotel ... the new Reno Hotel ... as a cadet catering hand, only——'

'Only?' Huw was asking again.

'Only I didn't know some necessary weights and I miscalculated some cooking times, and I——' Umberto looked down again.

'So after those two unproving flights you did that talking over with each other?' Huw's voice was careful now. 'Where did you do this talking over? Far away from the madding crowds, I presume. Some secluded park? Some cave?'

'Oh, no!' They were talking together again. 'Crossing the street.'

'From the hospital,' Jane provided, 'after I'd been rejected. Umberto was waiting for me.'

'From the hotel,' said Umberto. 'Jane was waiting to see how I got on.'

'We decided,' Jane took up, 'we'd been hasty, that we needed more behind us, that we'd come back here and take up again where we'd left off. If' ... nervously ... 'you would take me, Uncle Huw. If Umberto's parents would take him.'

'Very considerate of you,' Huw grunted.

'We would have been here hours ago,' Jane explained, 'only we ran out of gas. We had to walk then. I wanted Umberto to walk to his place, not double up by seeing me home first, but he said his parents had always told him to be a gentleman.'

'Which he is,' Manny broke in very forcibly, at the same time giving Huw a challenging look. 'And now' ... getting up ... *we're going to have coffee.* She proclaimed it in a no-arguing voice.

She cooked bacon and eggs, too, and the four of them sat round the table, and this time the children ate and talked as well. Huw had been right when he had said that bringing out and airing improved appetites, for, as confidences poured out, Manny had to pour more coffee, replenish plates.

'This is our only food since our school lunches,' mumbled Jane, stoking busily. 'Umberto's father's car is very bad on gas, and we had no money left.'

'My father,' came in Umberto anxiously, 'knows I can manage the car, Mr Grant. He knows, being under age, I would not do it just to show I can drive. He trusts me in that.'

'Do you think he'll trust you any more?' Huw asked.

'I think he will when I tell him.'

'What will you tell him?'

'That he was right when he said I should learn more, for I know now I should. I think when I tell him that, and tell him that the head chef of the new hotel also said it, he will see I am really serious in what I intend to do.'

'Care to tell me more, Umberto? For instance, what the head chef said?'

'He said' ... for the first time since the pair had come home they exchanged grins ... 'suffering snakes!'

'What?'

'He gave me a quick weight examination. He said that in good cooking there are no handfuls of this or touches of that, it all has to be in proper terms, and when I gave him my answer, he said——'

'Suffering snakes,' giggled Jane.

'Then he did the school bit, and how, if I was really serious, I was to have more than a dab hand with an omelette. He said that only then and not before would he want to see me again.' Umberto took a deep breath. 'I'm going to do what he says and he is going to see me again.'

'Jane?' Huw asked next.

'Much the same,' sighed Jane. 'Only I sat in Matron's office and did some sums and things.' A pause. 'I did awfully.'

'Suffering snakes?' asked Huw, not altering his face.

'Something of the sort. But Matron was quite nice about it. She said the spirit counts as well, and that it appeared I had that. All I would need to do would be to brush up, and I'm going to. I'm really going to get my head down. Manny, can I have another cup?'

'You won't sleep.'

'I'm so tired I'll sleep for ever. No, I won't, I mustn't miss tomorrow's school bus.'

'I'll see you don't,' Manny promised. She looked at Huw, her eyes telegraphing 'Umberto.'

'When you're ready, Umberto,' Huw complied, 'I'll run you into Elkington. I've already been on the phone with your father' ... had he? When? wondered Manny ... 'and he's anxious to have you back.'

'To lecture me,' Umberto accepted philosophically.

'No, as a matter of fact to help him in the café. It seems he's busy tonight and could do with another hand.'

'Dad said that? But he never lets me. Oh, I know I made the sandwiches the other day, but I knew he didn't like me doing it.'

'Well, he wants you there now.' It was Huw's turn to telegraph a message to Manny. She gave a flick back.

Umberto needed no more encouragement. He got up, thanked Manny for the meal, thanked Huw for driving him in, then, of all things, took and shook Jane's hand.

Of all things, very seriously Jane shook his in return.

As soon as the men had gone, Manny, anxious to get to the phone to ring the Fuccilis, suggested to Jane that she go to bed.

'I should help you clear up,' Jane protested.

'You'll help me more by waking up fresh in the morning and not having to be shaken awake.'

'I wanted to wait up to tell Uncle Huw I'm sorry.'

'I think the way you're acting now will say that.'

'I'm glad it's over.' Jane yawned happily. 'I don't think at heart I'm really naturally rash after all.'

'Like Judy.' It was out before Manny could stop it.

'Yes.'

Manny took the dishes to the sink and poured on hot water. Making it sound as casual as she could, she asked: 'Who was Judy?'

'You asked me that before, Manny. She was the family's rash one—I told you.'

'Yes, you did, Jane. An aunt, I think you said.'

'That's right.' Jane yawned again.

'What happened?' Manny whirled in detergent, trying to pretend only a passing interest.

'It's never clear. No one ever really says. As a matter of fact, Manny, I don't think anyone really knows.'

'Not know!'

'That's true. From what little ears——'

'Big ears,' corrected Manny with a grin.

'Could hear,' laughed Jane, 'this Judy just went. Manny, if you're sure I can't help I *will* go to bed.'

'I'm sure, Jane.' Manny smiled her off.

She went at once to the telephone and rang the White Rose, had a session ... quite a successful one ... with Mr. Fuccili, then came back to the kitchen sink.

But there action stopped. Instead of washing the dishes, Manny stood staring in front of her. She was thinking of Judy who 'just went.'

CHAPTER TEN

MANNY was drying the final dish when Huw's car pulled up at the cottage. Several moments later he knocked on the door. The subdued tap indicated that he was not sure whether she still would be up, and a glance at the clock shocked her. Had she really been that long at the sink? She knew she had stood staring at the water, swirling it around with a dish mop, all the time wondering about Huw and his deep ... too deep? ... concern for his niece. She knew she had been thinking of Judy. Judy, the rash one.

She let Huw in and nodded him to a chair, but he shook his head.

'It's time you were in bed,' he said.

'You, too.'

'Yes,' he sighed, 'it's been one hell of a day. And Larry didn't help.'

'Don't you rather over-react there?' (In that *as well*, Manny could have added.)

'No, Emmanuelle, Larry is my natural enemy. He knows it, I know it. Society has made it like that.'

'There was no trouble under Peter,' she pointed out.

'Also nothing happened under Peter. That's why I had to come.'

'You mean you were directed to Soleil Bay for a specific reason?'

'Yes,' said Huw.

'But if nothing had happened——'

'Nothing had happened profit-wise,' he said flatly.

Manny looked at him with undisguised distaste.

'So you're not a human trouble-shooter as I thought but a money one?'

'Of course. What else should a firm require? However, the human angle is ever present, and particularly in any kind of trouble. Are you answered, Miss Trouble?'

'I'm sorry,' Manny gritted, 'I didn't want to be a trouble. You ... no, it would be your firm, wouldn't it ... have been considerate to me,' she said stiffly.

He gave the stiff apology a stiff response.

'Think nothing of it. I just called in to tell you that all is well on the Fuccili front.'

'Oh, thank you!' Happiness for Umberto pushed aside Manny's irritation.

'No, thank yourself. From what I've gathered your few words earlier with Papa Fuccili were very telling words. I believe you informed him that one day he might have a master chef for a son, something much more important than a mere clerk. I believe he heard from you that the money would be better, the demand greater, and the self-satisfaction for Umberto beyond estimation.'

'Well——' demurred Manny modestly.

'Anyway, it bore fruit. Gradually Mr Fuccili's worship of offices began to diminish. In the end he wouldn't have changed the humblest cooking range for the most expensive computer, and when I tactfully pointed out that Umberto would never have become a computer operator, anyway, he couldn't wait for his son to follow the family calling.'

'Though not too soon, I trust,' Manny worried. 'You heard Umberto report——'

'Suffering snakes? Yes. Oh, no, I think when Umberto tells his father that that chef doesn't want him until he can pass his exams then everything will be right.' Huw paused, then looked a little wistfully at Manny. 'Will everything be right with Jane, too?'

'I expect so.' Manny hung up the towel.

Huw stood waiting for more than that, waiting for reassurance, and Manny knew he was disappointed with her apparent lack of interest.

She *was* interested, very deeply so, but somehow she could not tell him. She knew she had to know more first, more about Judy, more about the situation, more about Huw Grant. Only then could she really share his concern and worry. But when she didn't know, and when he would not tell her ...

'Goodnight.' Manny half waited for him to hold her back ... confide in her ...

But—— 'Goodnight,' he said and left.

Jane resumed school the next morning and by the end of the week the episode never might have happened. Manny was relieved when Jane's new learning dedication began to wear off after a while; too much of a thing could result in nothing at all, she knew. The Jane that at last emerged was the average schoolgirl, blow-hot, blow-cold, full of enthusiasms, devoid of them, practical one day, full of dreams the next. Continuously in love.

There is this gorgeous prefect, Manny, Jane raved, absolutely dishy. Later it was a junior teacher. Then of all people the Head. Then came Julian.

'Julian Winthrop—he's a sweetie.'

'What subject does he teach?' asked Manny.

'He doesn't teach. He's an author. He's living in the district for a time to get some local colour.'

'How did you meet him, Jane?'

'We didn't meet, we encountered.' Jane's voice grew dreamy.

'Where?'

'The coffee shop. You know, Manny, the White Rose.'

'I don't know whether your uncle would like that, Jane,' said Manny doubtfully.

'But there were a dozen of us, Manny. Umberto makes wizard pancakes, he works at the café after school. Our class patronises him whenever we have the money. It doesn't cost much. What did you do today, Manny?' Jane examined Manny's canvas.

'Oh,' Jane said with obvious sincerity, 'that's good.'

'Do you think so?' Manny was pleased.

'Oh, yes, I can see what you're after, so it must be good, for I'm not clever at seeing things. I told Julian that. I was talking about you and your gift. He would understand, being a writer.'

'The next panel will be the destruction part,' Manny said, only half listening as she always did to Jane's chatter.

'Yes, and that will be hard,' Jane sympathised. 'I told Julian and he agreed that destruction is always difficult to portray.'

'He sounds very knowing.'

'Oh, he is. You'd like him, Manny.'

'I'm sure. But I wouldn't keep on about him, not in front of your uncle.'

'Because of the rash one,' Jane surmised shrewdly.

'Yes, Jane,' Manny said with a slight smile. Where, she asked herself, was Huw's 'bird brain' now?

Though everything seemed settled regarding Jane, Manny learned in the days that followed that Huw Grant was not treading the same easy path. Every company had its troubles, she knew, but Peter, the former boss, had seemed to have a charmed passage.

'Because,' Manny's father always had said when the subject had arisen, 'old Pete was on the way out and not worrying any more.'

But Huw Grant was younger, and he did worry ... worry everyone else, according to Larry, who visited Manny often. Larry added that the men did not like it.

'Of all things Grant is making it a closed camp, Manny.'

'Is he allowed to do a thing like that?' she queried.

'I believe he's a legal man as well as an executive, so no doubt he has all the answers.'

'What exactly do you mean by a closed camp, Larry?'

'No open gates any more for anyone to come in or go out.'

'Jane and I have always been forbidden to go in and out.'

'Oh, yes,' Larry grinned, 'but that was done because of the kid—well, kid as she is now. The way she was before, all eyeshadow and come-hither, I reckon Grant did the right thing. But I wasn't meaning you, I was meaning us. Locked gates! None of the old come and go!'

'Has Mr Grant given a reason?'

'No.' Larry added with his usual truculence: 'Bosses don't.'

Manny said thoughtfully: 'Yes, I suppose the men wouldn't care for it. It would make them feel they were at school.'

'Or in jail,' Larry said more forcefully. 'Grant

wants to wake up if he doesn't like repercussions.'

'You mean strikes?'

'It could happen,' he shrugged.

'It hasn't so far.'

'We had Peter then.'

'And weren't functioning as you should.'

Larry looked quizzically at Manny. 'Whose side are you on, young Manny?'

They both laughed.

But Manny was serious when she approached Huw the next day.

'I've finished the first mural panel,' she announced.

'Yes. I've seen it.'

'You've seen it! You mean you went in uninvited?'

'I am your employer, remember, not your guest.'

'I'll remember that.' Manny could not resist tacking on: 'I hope your other employees remember.'

'They'll remember,' he said coolly. 'Anyway, why the objection about the studio? It's not the cottage, it's not private.'

'But the entirety is mine—I mean it's my lease.'

'Is it?' he came back quickly, but at once he dropped that. 'Yes, I saw the mural and it's everything I would ask.' A pause. 'Anything else, Miss Norbert?'

'Yes, Mr Grant, I want to do some sketches *inside* the works.'

'Naturally you would need to do that,' he agreed.

'Then how do I get in?'

'Oh, I see Larry's been talking to you.'

'Yes, about your closed camp.'

'As usual he makes mountains out of molehills.

I've merely made the camp less free and easy.' Huw added laconically: 'I did it for the men's own good.'

'How could that be?'

He looked at her levelly. 'There were instances of pilfering.'

Manny stared incredulously back at him, and he repeated himself. 'Money has been missing from pockets.'

'But——'

'But it could have happened inside, you're thinking?'

'Yes ... though I hate to think it.'

'So would I hate it, and I'm glad to tell you I don't have to, because ever since the gates and doors were closed the wretched business ceased.'

Manny was silent for a while.

'All the same, the men have not liked being restricted,' she warned.

'Also all the same, they're now able to leave their coats hanging around and come back to find the contents of their wallets still intact.'

'Those are strong words, and closing a camp is a strong action,' she insisted.

'I feel strongly about this,' he assured her. 'My office was entered a few nights ago.'

'Before you started locking up?'

'Yes. That was the real reason I did it.'

'Was anything taken?'

'A plan.'

'Oh, no money, then.' Manny shrugged, but her nonchalance did not last long.

'You little fool,' Huw burst out angrily, 'this plan

was worth more than money, it meant——' He stopped abruptly, obviously curbing himself.

'It meant some future sources of household paint?' Manny scorned, for she knew that the titanium gained from the rutile went to that purpose.

He did not speak for some minutes, and when he did he did not answer her question.

'Fortunately I discovered the theft early enough to act,' he said. 'Every venue I'd marked down is now pre-secured.'

'*Sand* pre-secured?' She gave a little laugh.

Again he did not answer her.

'So doors are locked for that,' Manny persisted.

'And for money taken out of pockets,' he reminded her drily, but he still did not answer her questions.

Manny gave an uncaring shrug. 'Well, it makes no difference to us, to Jane and to me, we were always locked out.'

'Jane was, and you know why. Now she can come in if she likes. After being seen in pigtails and panama——' He laughed.

'I doubt if she's interested,' Manny said meanly. 'She's told me you're all as old as the hills.'

Huw looked at her narrowly. 'Your opinion, too?'

'Does it matter?'

'Who knows?' He gave a hunch of his big shoulders. 'However, *you* were never included in the veto. You must have known that.'

'I didn't know.'

'Then you know now.' He reached into his pocket and produced a key. 'Come and go as you please.'

'Thank you, I will. Well, until I have what I need.'

'There's no time limit,' he said quietly. 'The key is for all time.'

'I'll return it when I have what I want.'

'I won't be asking for it, Emmanuelle.' He gave her a long look.

The next morning, after she had dropped Jane at the crossroads and returned home again, Manny took out her sketchbook and crossed to the works. The gates were secured as was the rule now, but she unlocked them and went in.

She walked round the diggings, avoiding the danger sections at present under mining, yet retreating only as far as not to be a hindrance. She sketched, jotted down reminders, made notes. After that she left again, carefully locking up behind her, then hurried to get her impressions on to the canvas while they were still fresh in her mind. In her absorption she worked all day, even forgetting to eat. She only remembered Jane when she happened to look up at the clock. She saw that she should have left for the crossroads an hour ago. She went at once, and Jane was waiting, the bus, Jane pointing out unnecessarily, having already deposited her and gone on.

'But not to worry,' Jane reassured Manny, 'I haven't been here long. The timetable is altered, we're leaving later. From now on you can pick me up at five instead of four.'

Still caught up with her work, Manny nodded.

She was pleased with the progress of the second panel, Soleil Bay as it now was. She was gratified when Jane exclaimed when she saw it that it looked like moon country. It was the effect she wanted, and she found herself waiting with an eagerness she would not have admitted for Huw's reaction.

However, he did not come over to react. Jane told her that things were not going well at the works, so Manny put his absence down to that. 'But how do you know, Jane?' she asked.

'Grapevine, I suppose.' Jane changed the subject.

Manny dabbled for a few more days, then, deciding that since Huw was commissioning the mural he should at least see it, she went across and let herself in with the key she had not yet returned.

It was late afternoon when she went, shadows rapidly overcoming day's final resistance. The men were all inside the barracks, relaxing over beers, watching television, playing cards. It was very quiet.

Manny made for the small separate hut belonging to the boss, then, seeing it shut, she decided that Huw was either with the others or in the office. Keeping in mind what Jane had said about the climate just now within the project, she turned in the direction of the office. There was no light on, but at this indefinite time of late day no light was actually necessary. Manny tapped on the door.

She thought she heard something inside. It was very light as if someone was moving very carefully. She tapped again, but there was no sound at all now. She went to tap a third time—then abruptly she was caught, whirled around, then hurried from where she waited at the door. It was Huw holding her arms and pushing her, and he was very angry.

'Damn you, Manny, what in tarnation are you doing? Why did you have to turn up at this very moment?'

They were well away from the office now, and Manny shook herself free of Huw.

'Why not? I came to ask you to look over what I've been doing on the mural, seeing after all that you commissioned it. But if it's too much trouble——'

'Of course I'll look at it. Denounce it, too, if it needs it. But did you have to arrive just then?'

She looked at him shrewdly. 'Is there fresh trouble?'

'No, the same trouble.'

'An uninvited guest?'

'Yes.'

'Then I'm very sorry. Shouldn't you go back at once and see if you can run the offender down, this quite remarkable offender who laughs at locked gates?'

'During the day a door has to open some time, so he could have got in then.'

'He? I thought trouble for you came from females, Mr Grant. You called me Miss Trouble.'

He did not banter back. He said quite grimly: 'In this instance I believe the trouble is male.'

She started an edged smile, but at once he snapped: '*I'm* not laughing, Miss Norbert.'

'Nor am I, instead I'm wondering why you're wasting time if you really think someone broke into your office.' Deliberately Manny kept to herself the noise she believed she had heard. 'I'm wondering,' she went on, 'why you're not doubling back.'

'To surprise someone who might still be there, the

person having obligingly remained for me? Use your sense!'

'You're always at pains to tell me I have none,' she retorted.

'Have I said that? But' ... with a quick, totally unexpected change ... 'I could never say you have no hands.' He surprised Manny by taking both her hands in his. 'You see, I *have* looked at the next panel, Manny.'

The sudden difference in him baffled her. She stammered: 'When did you see it? Why didn't you tell me?'

'I went across after you took Jane to the bus this morning.'

'And?'

'And this,' he said simply. He turned each hand over and kissed each palm in turn, and the effect on Manny was almost shattering. She never had had her hands kissed before and she could not have believed that such an old-world tribute would leave her so awakened. She lifted her eyes from her hands that he still held and met Huw's silver glance. Silver was always a cool colour, but now the silver glowed warmly. She looked quickly down again.

'Manny——' he began.

'I'm glad you liked the work,' she said jerkily. 'Tomorrow I'm going up to the headland to sketch the ruination from there. Jane calls what I've done moon country.' She knew she was chattering, and was annoyed with herself, but she could not take her eyes away from the hands he still held. She could not look up and meet that *warm* silver glance.

He released her hands and stepped back, saying nothing. Embarrassed now, Manny went back to the cottage.

Manny did climb the headland the next day. Having deposited Jane she came back to the house, put a flask of tea and a sandwich in a bag with her sketch pad and was soon recording the devastation that man and machines can make to loveliness.

She worked inspired until hunger caught up with her, then she stopped for a meal. She was pleased with her morning, and lay back after she had finished, tired but replete. She did not know at what stage she fell asleep.

She woke with a start. Everything around her was quiet, so she wondered why she was jumping to her feet as she was, almost as though someone had called to her and the sound penetrated her oblivion. But there was nothing at all, except . . . and Manny looked down and around from the advantage of the cliff . . . far in the distance the school bus approaching the crossroads where she picked up Jane. Good gracious, it couldn't be that time, she must have slept for hours. She looked at her watch and saw that it was. Jane would be waiting for her.

Then she saw, and was a little dismayed, that the bus had not stopped, that no one had got out. At once her mind went to the last time Jane had not been on the bus, and she groaned. But she was not over-worried, she felt confident that Jane would never do the same thing twice. Nonetheless she had better hurry down.

It was then that the call came, and was *consciously*

heard this time. The first call must have awakened her, but this call alerted her.

Manny followed the sound to the edge of the cliff.

CHAPTER ELEVEN

She crept as near as she dared to the commencement of the drop, then peered over. All she could see was the base of the cliff, after that a narrow strip of sand only visible when a wave retreated, then sea, then more sea.

Every time a wave ran up the sand and boomed against the rock base there was a thunder of sound, but after the wave retreated again there was silence. Except, Manny puzzled, when a call broke the silence, like the call she had just heard. She peered again, quite perilously this time, then lay down and wriggled herself cautiously to the edge. From there she could focus better, and she noted that the narrow strip of beach became narrower with each successive wave, and she knew that the tide was coming in.

She closed her eyes a moment to clear her vision, for the salt was stinging her lids, but when she looked again it was still the same scene, except for a neck-lace of gulls making flight patterns above the ocean and against the cliff face. She followed them a moment, caught up in the beauty of their movement as they paused on the swelling sea, then rose to hover above the jagged rocks. She must have imagined the distress call, she mused, for there was still only a setting of gulls, sky and sea.

And a figure.

A man stretched prone near the base of the rocks directly beneath her; he was only a few feet from the rising surf. Even as Manny watched she saw one of the larger waves break across his legs. She looked to the sea, then looked to the rocks above him. She felt he could be caught. Surely he must be asleep, or very inattentive, not to have realised that himself. She cupped her mouth with her hands and shouted as loudly as she could. She could not have said if she called anything specific, she only knew she screamed out and put everything into that scream.

It reached him. He looked up at her from his prone position and Manny saw he was Huw Grant. At once he shouted back, but the wind was against him and she could not catch a word. But she could tell why he was not removing himself : *it was because he could not.* He was indicating downward to his leg or ankle. Manny did not wait for any more, she wriggled back to safety, got to her feet, then raced along to an opening in the headland that she had used as a child. It was a dizzy drop, she recalled, probably dizzier now that she was older and aware of danger, but it did lead down to the cove.

The urgency of getting there as soon as she could at least rid her of any adult hesitancy, and, ignoring the quite formidable steepness of the descent, she took a deep breath, stepped out, started down. From lack of use the track was barely discernible, and she slipped several times. She also suffered scratches from the harsh gorses, cuts from the edges of rocks.

Eight feet from the base, where some rough steps had once taken over, she found there was no longer any descent. She paused a moment, then jumped.

She was jarred by the impact, and for a moment stood catching her breath. She was still breathing unevenly when she looked up and saw the big wave bearing down on her, one of those ferocious boomers that irregularly occur in an incoming tide. It seemed to be racing directly at her, and it bore down so quickly there was nothing to do about it, no time to run, no time to try to clamber up the cliff. As she was whirled over and over she hoped that Huw, higher up, heavier than she was, was not suffering the same onslaught.

As the wave sucked away at last she looked quickly across to Huw, but instead of the man she saw spray, spray from another boomer, even higher than the last. Though she moved quickly she was still caught, flung at the base, then dragged into deep water. Once there new waves piled over her, rotating her in boiling turbulence. She was drawn under, then up again, forced to the rocks, then carried back to the sea once more. The thing she had come to do, to stop Huw Grant from being claimed by the sea, seemed now to be happening to her. Huw. Huw! She said it in a choking breath as she receded again. Huw, help me!

His voice came fairly *pulling* her in. He shouted: 'I can't come to get you, but I can see another wave coming. Relax and come with it. Come to me!'

She did not answer, there was no time. She rose in the wave, began the horrible backwash again ...

except that this time a hand caught her. She felt the backwash taking them both, then his weight, with hers, thwarted the sea, and the wave ran out again.

'Are you all right, Manny?' She heard his voice, but only faintly.

'Yes.'

'Then for heaven's sake get further up the rock. We're not finished. Drag me after you.'

'But you're hurt.'

'I'll be drowned if you don't act. Shove me, push me, roll me. Take no notice if I yell. There'll be one more boomer, I'd say, that's the pattern of the tide, then after that we'll only have a regular rise, which we should survive. Now *push*!'

Manny did. She heard a sharp gasp, looked down and saw that he was white with pain. At that moment Huw's final boomer broke. She waited till it had spent its violence and withdrew again.

'You were right,' she gasped after a long moment of waiting for more.

'They go in sequences of seven,' he said, 'and I've been counting.'

They both lay in exhausted silence for a while.

Huw broke the silence. He demanded: 'Why are you here?'

'To help you, of course.' Manny stopped, embarrassed. As it had happened he had had to help her. But he had still called to her, she remembered.

'You shouted for me to come, you indicated you couldn't move because you were hurt,' she said truculently.

'I shouted for you to *get* help, not play the heroine.

I can't imagine what fool impulse brought you sliding down yourself, unless——' He flicked a look at her.

She would not meet that look. She said briskly: 'Just tell me if you're safe enough to leave and I'll climb back and get that help.'

'You'll do nothing of the sort. Descending in blind enthusiasm is easier than ascending without any driving force. Also, if you look up you'll see you would first have to scale the base rock where before you simply leapt and landed.'

'It wasn't simple,' Manny said feelingly. 'I was jarred.'

'It should be barred, not jarred—girls like you are a menace. Now we're both stuck here.'

'We can't be!' Manny said, aghast.

'Let me finish. We're stuck here until the tide goes out again.'

'We can't be.' Manny repeated that, but she had glanced up quickly, and she knew he was right. Although she had descended there was no hope of her climbing up again. She would never overcome, not unaided, those first straight eight feet. She sat silent.

'When you said "stuck here",' she asked at last, 'were you meaning that the only way to get help is to walk round the bluff for it? Wait on the tide to do so?'

'Well, I wasn't asking you to fly,' he shrugged.

'How long will the tide take?'

'I think we can say there'll be no more boomers, that we're at the peak. Leave an hour for full water, then add six hours for ebb and slack water, then——'

'What?' Manny broke in aghast.

'I said six for ebb and slack. But of course you would know that.'

'Yes, I knew, but——'

'But you never thought you'd meet it. Well, start to meet it now. We have seven hours in front of us, plus at least three hours more for enough light for you to see your way back, because you couldn't go in the dark. In my young days three and seven added up to ten. Did it in yours?'

'Stop making a joke of it!' she said crossly.

'A joke,' he grimaced, and he looked down at his leg.

Manny followed the direction, and asked: 'How did you do it? Is it bad?'

'I was on the track of some promising evidence.'

'Rutile?'

He did not answer that, instead he continued: 'I was looking for something but didn't look where I was going. No, I don't think it will threaten my life. But I'll certainly need to be helped out of this wretched situation.' He looked around him and groaned.

'It could have been worse still,' Manny reminded. 'A wave could have taken you.'

'No, I was safe enough, I'd previously estimated that I would be out of danger.'

'But you were nearly washed off with me.'

'Only because I rolled myself down *for* you.' He looked at her and grinned, but Manny was silent.

'I suppose I must say thank you,' she mumbled presently.

'Meanwhile finding it hard when you thought I'd

be saying thank you to you? Let's leave it at that,
then, shall we? at both of us being thankful to each
other. Let us consider instead how we're going to
spend the next ten hours.'

But Manny knew she could not consider that.

'The camp?' she asked hopefully.

'Won't even notice my absence. I often eat away
from the mess these days. Gerry will leave a tray at
the door and only find out the next morning that it
hasn't been touched. What about Jane! Could she
start something?'

'Jane is very accepting, she'll think I'm out sketching, get her meal, do her homework, go to bed. She's
a heavy sleeper.'

'So much for help from outside.' Huw hunched
his shoulders. 'Now let's think of ourselves. Will you
be cold?'

'I don't think so, by the sea is always warm.'

'Hungry?'

'I had a meal at noon. Will you be?'

'I won't dwell on it,' he said feelingly.

'Is your leg paining?' Manny asked.

'Only when I move it, which unhappily I have to—
I have an abominable cramp.'

'Can I do something?'

'You can edge the leg into a different position for
me. I'll wince, but ignore it, it has to be done.' He
lay back and Manny did the edging over of the
cramped limb. He flinched, but obviously tried to
hide it from her, so she pretended not to notice.

'Perhaps a passing boat will see us,' she said—
foolishly, for there was no fishing fleet at Soleil, and
the big ship routes were too far out.

'Any discovery of us will have to be soon,' Huw said drily, 'it'll be dark in less than an hour.'

'Is it that late? I know I fell asleep after lunch ...' Manny's voice trailed off. She was remembering waking and looking around her, seeing in the distance the school bus go by the crossroads without stopping. She glanced hesitantly at Huw, but decided not to tell him.

He had seen her look, though. He sighed: 'What trauma is it now? The idea of lying side by side with me until morning?'

'I won't be doing that.'

'Then you'll find it very hard sitting up all night.'

Manny only sat straighter.

She sat like that, making occasional conversation with him, for the next hour. Then, darkness gathering them in, she began a determined game of I Spy.

'I spy,' Huw joined in, 'U–F.'

'I think you mean U–F–O.'

'No, U–F. Ultimate fate.'

'Meaning?'

'Meaning give in, Manny, you can't keep this up, sit back if you can't lie back. At least relax.'

'No.' But Manny did lower herself a few inches. She went a little further back several minutes after. Presently she was lying by his side.

There was little talk between them during the dark hour before the first star pricked through. Huw seemed in a world of his own, Manny was content to listen to the soft wash of the tide, for the boom had gone out of the sea now, and only the sibilance of withdrawal remained. Manny supposed she must have withdrawn, too, for when Huw spoke to her some time later, as well as the evening star the moon had emerged.

'Romantic, isn't it?' he said. 'Did you ever do this with Justin Welsh?'

'Did I ever do what?'

'I don't know, Emmanuelle. Tell me. Did you?'

'If you're going to go on like that I'll——'

'You'll go away? Where?'

'The tide must be down a lot further by now,' she said evasively.

'You won't notice any diffierence for a long time yet. No, we're still trapped. But don't worry, I promise not to question you. Except——'

Manny sighed: 'Except?'

'Except haven't you ever, don't you ever, think of him? Think of Welsh?'

Manny was silent. She wondered what Huw would say if she answered No. It would sound unbelievable, it was unbelievable, but since her return to Soleil she had not thought of Justin. He had flicked across her mind when she had seen someone like him at Elkington that day, but apart from then ...

'You must have thought about him,' Huw persisted, 'after all, he'd asked you to marry him and you'd said Yes.' He waited a moment, then when Manny did not speak he went on: 'At least you must have *wondered*.'

'Wondered?' she queried.

'Wondered why, in spite of my ruling, he hadn't tried to see you. Love' ... a wry note in his voice ... 'is supposed to seek.'

Again Manny was silent.

'Or *has* he contacted you?' Huw persisted again.

She decided to answer that. 'No,' she said.

'Then you've contacted him?'

'No.'

A few minutes went by.

'Manny' ... Huw's voice was gentle now ... 'were you very hurt?'

She said stiffly, not wanting him to know the truth: 'What would you think?'

'I don't know. I can only answer for him, knowing his poor capacity for being hurt.'

'Knowing that by merely being his employer?' Manny said with scorn.

'Yes ... and something else.' She looked quickly at him, but at once he continued, 'I know about Welsh, but I don't know about you. Would you tell me?'

She became silent again, and presently he sighed and started on another channel.

'This mishap' ... he looked down at his leg ... 'couldn't have happened at a worse time. Headquarters are plaguing me for results, and the men are being difficult. They need my eye on them just now.'

'You're fearing you won't be able to cast that eye?'

'Lying in a cot as I feel certain I shall be lying, no. But the moment I can hobble I'll be on the job again. There's a spirit of dissatisfaction, no doubt induced by——'

'By Larry, you're going to say. You have a fixation about Larry.'

'As a matter of interest, your interest, I was referring to your ex-fiancé. I was going to cite Welsh.'

'Whatever for? Poor Justin isn't even here.'

'But he was here, and some of the effect still remains. Only when I rid the camp of that can I hope to right things. Larry could help, but of course he won't.'

'For the reason he doesn't like you?' Manny baited.

'I prefer to say he doesn't like the system. But he's an intelligent fellow and one day ... But Manny, *Manny,* what in heaven are we doing talking shop like this? Look at that sea!'

Manny looked, looked at the gold and silver of it, gold where the moon sent its beams, silver where the stars were reflected.

'... Yes, it's lovely,' she conceded in spite of herself.

'As you are lovely, Emmanuelle,' Huw said suddenly, unexpectedly. Forgetting his pain in movement, he turned to her. 'I've watched you, Manny, watched you from the day I first saw you, sometimes I think I've never stopped watching you. Manny, you're the loveliest, dearest thing.'

Manny did not speak.

'Manny,' Huw went on, 'I want that loveliest and dearest. I need it. I must have it. I have to have you. That's why I brought up the subject of Welsh. I can't believe that anything remains with you and Welsh, but if it does I want to know. I have to learn how to reach you with him standing between us. Tell me, Manny.'

His hand reached out and touched her hair, then it moved from her hair to her neck and then to her throat. Presently she could feel it resting on her breast.

'*Tell me, Manny,*' he said again.

Manny put trembling fingers to her lips. All at once she needed to stop a torrent of eager words. They were aching in her, they were hard to stem, it was all she could do to stop herself shouting them. Every fibre of her was urging her to answer: 'Justin doesn't stand between us, no one does. *No one, Huw.*'

But she did stop. It was only the gold and silver doing all this to her, she reminded herself, only a beautiful night. As for him, as for Huw Grant, the man faced long painful hours, and she promised a possible pleasant diversion from his suffering. Ordinarily this situation would never have occurred, and she refused to be carried foolishly away by a moon, stars, sea—and two close, far too close, silver eyes. She tried to turn away.

He caught her, held her, forced her back. 'Not too far, you'll fall off,' he warned.

'After what's happened today there can't be much worse.'

'No? Not even this?' As he laughed he kissed her. He kissed her hair, her eyes, her ears and finally her mouth. For a diversion, Manny told herself suffocatingly, he was playing the part to the full.

She tried to pull back, but his clasp was too tight, she tried to avoid his lips, but he overpowered her. She lay quietly under his caresses, hoping that her lack of response would at last convey itself to him, discourage him, but at some stage, she could not have said why, her resistance left her, and she was kissing him back. She tried to stiffen herself, but failed. When he drew her nearer she came to him readily.

Finally she drifted into oblivion that way: in his arms. When she woke it was first light of dawn, and she was still in his arms.

She disentangled herself carefully, she could tell he was deeply asleep.

She clambered down to the now wide strip of beach, and in the bright morning she found her way round the headland, and then, out of sight of Huw, she ran back over the sands to the camp.

CHAPTER TWELVE

MANNY was breathless by the time she reached the works and picked her way around the mining devastation up to the huddle of dormitories and huts. She had not thought the camp would be accessible, so had been prepared to shout her way in, but when she gave a passing push to the side entrance, the gate answered her pressure. It was the same gate to which Huw had given her a key, and the key was still across at the cottage. The gate should have been locked, she knew she had left it secured, so apparently someone after her had either forgotten the new order or deliberately disobeyed it. She recalled how Huw had said that the men were being unco-operative. Putting conjectures aside, she went straight to the main dormitory and knocked on the door. When it was unanswered she banged.

One of the men, still in his pyjama pants, opened the door angrily and was about to abuse Manny when he recognised her and grinned instead.

'I thought you were the boss. How did you get in?'

'Through a gate.'

'Can't be done, we're locked in every night like a boarding school.'

'I'm here, aren't I?' she retorted.

'Looks like you, Manny. Anything wrong?'

'A lot.' Manny paused. 'With your boss.'

'Then there's nothing wrong,' the man said stonily.

Manny actually stamped her foot at him. 'Don't be stupid, Les' ... she had known Les for years ... 'this is an emergency!'

At once, to give Les his due, he became serious.

'Sorry, Manny. Where is he? Will I need some help?'

'He's at the base of the headland. We've been there all night.' Manny flushed, realising that that was something she could have left unsaid. 'I mean,' she endeavoured, 'Mr Grant has. I was walking round and I found him ... Thank you, Les.' For Les was patting her shoulder encouragingly and turning back to the dormitory.

'Rise and shine,' he bellowed, 'there's trouble!' When there was no response he raised his voice and spelt out trouble letter by letter. He advised Manny to clear out before she saw more than she should.

Manny walked round while she waited for them.

Her steps, intentionally or by accident, took her to the executive unit, and, just as Huw had said, last night's meal was still on a tray outside the door. She frowned. It had always been a very amenable body here, no unpleasantness as there seemed now. She heard her name called, and turned. As usual Larry had taken over.

'What is it, young Manny?' Larry asked.

'Mr Grant. He fell yesterday and had to spend the night under the cliff. Fortunately he could haul himself away from danger, but he'll need help to get out now.'

'Done,' nodded Larry, tactfully not asking any more questions. 'You, Les. You, Bill. You, Jack. You, Clem.' He turned again to Manny. 'Stretcher job?'

'It's a leg injury.' Manny was aware that she was flushing furiously.

'Bring the stretcher,' nodded Larry to his selected helpers.

'Shall I come to show you?' Manny asked.

For the briefest of moments Larry's eyes took in her dishevelment.

'Best hop home and run a bath,' he advised.

Manny nodded, then thankfully went.

Jane was still asleep, and Manny had had her bath and dressed before the girl sauntered out to the kitchen.

'Sorry I couldn't stop up last night, Manny,' she yawned, 'I was so tired I turned in early. You must have got on to some good sketching material. Were you very late?'

'Late enough,' Manny avoided, and Jane yawned again and accepted that answer. As it didn't seem the right time to ask Jane why she hadn't returned yesterday in the school bus, Manny got the breakfast while Jane showered, then later drove her to the crossroads.

'Do you want me to pick you up this afternoon?' Manny asked with careful casualness. 'I was detained yesterday.'

'Gathering material,' nodded Jane. 'I guessed that when I got out of the bus and didn't see you, so I set off by myself. It isn't all that far to the cottage from the crossroads, and it's a pleasant walk.' Her lie was delivered very convincingly, but Manny, knowing that the bus had not stopped yesterday, was unconvinced.

'But,' continued Jane, 'when you pick me up this afternoon don't forget our new schedule, it's almost an hour later.'

'Yes, you told me.' The bus lumbered along, Jane got in and the bus left again. Manny returned to her car and drove uneasily back to Soleil. Something, she knew, was wrong.

Manny supposed that by now Huw had been duly returned to the works, his injury attended to, and either bed or a chair prescribed. She would have liked to have checked, but felt too embarrassed. Larry's tact had been appreciated, Les's, too, but men were still men, and Manny had no illusions as to what was being exchanged between them, in a kindly spirit no doubt, but still spoken. She squirmed.

However, she exchanged a few thoughts with herself during the day. She tried to work, but her fingers would not obey her, so eventually she threw her brushes down and went and sat on the verandah. Her mind ran in a hundred streams, but always came back to the same source: Huw's arms around her, Huw holding her not just for a protective moment but a protective night, the harbour of those arms. But she did find time to consider this morning's unlocked gate, and to wonder. Huw Grant had made the closing of the camp a new, rigid rule, yet still an entry had been available. Should she tell Huw when she saw him?

When would she see him?

Deliberately she kept out of sight of the camp for the rest of the day. She was not so unworldly as not to know that the men were smiling at each other. They all liked and respected her, she felt sure of that, but they were—men.

She collected Jane in the afternoon, a Jane already waiting for her. Also a rather quiet Jane, for which Manny was grateful. She had no wish to go over yesterday's happenings should Jane ask her.

But she should have known that she would discover. The following day the girl returned from school and at once enquired about her Uncle Huw.

'He had an accident,' she burst out, 'he was found at the bottom of a cliff. Really, Manny, you might have told me, not wait for me to find out!'

'He wasn't badly hurt, Jane,' Manny assured her. 'Only his leg.'

'Poor dear, suffering all by himself over there!'

'With fifty other men, and I don't think he's

actually suffering, he's just inconvenienced for a while. Also if it had been serious I would most certainly have told you.'

Jane, unsatisfied, declared: 'I'm going over.'

'No, Jane, you know you're forbidden to.'

'That was when I was—well, that was pre-school. Now I'm just a kid again and no femme fatale. Finally he's family, Manny, and no one is going to stop me.'

'The works are kept locked. It's a new rule.'

'I know a way,' said Jane, then stopped abruptly. If she had a guilty look, Manny did not see it, for at once the girl started down the hall.

'Jane!' Manny called, but Jane was gone. It was not long before she returned, and immediately she sought out Manny.

'Uncle Huw has to be brought over here, Manny,' she declared.

'He wouldn't want to be over here.'

'Want it, or not, he still must. He's not being looked after.'

'It's a leg injury, not a dangerous affliction. Don't make something out of nothing.'

'He needs looking after, Manny, you must go over and tell the men to bring him across.'

'Your uncle is perfectly all right, Jane,' insisted Manny.

'He's perfectly *neglected*. His meals left at the door!'

'Presumably he can reach them.'

'Manny, what's got into you?' burst out Jane. 'He's ill, he's——'

'He's temporarily incapacitated, Jane.'

'Yes, incapacitated, and left like that all night and day.'

'Did he say so?' asked Manny.

'... No, but I could see he was.'

'What did he say, Jane?' Manny persisted shrewdly.

'He said "Clear out",' Jane had to admit. 'But, Manny, he looked awful. You must do something.'

'I can't. We're not allowed over there.' Manny found herself grateful for that excuse. The thought of crossing to the camp and meeting the men's half-smiling, *knowing* looks appalled her.

'All right, if he dies it's on your hands!'

'Oh, Jane!' Manny gave up.

But it was no good, and in the end, though hating it, she went over.

The gates were all locked now, and she had forgotten the key, but a few calls got over that. Head high, Manny crossed to the executive hut. She knocked, waited for Huw's signal to go in, then went in.

Huw was lying on his bed, and he did not try to get up. Was he *unable* to get up? Manny feared for a worrying moment.

'So you do come here,' he remarked, but Manny did not answer. In spite of herself she could not feel indifference, for Jane was right. Huw definitely looked worse than he should look.

'I think you'd better come over to the cottage,' she told him.

He stared back at her in mock shock. 'And earn

you more raised eyebrows? My dear girl, you're already being spoken about, something that still, even in these modern days, evidently happens. At least' ... a sly glance ... 'when a young lady spends a night with a feller.' He held up his two hands in pretended dismay. As Manny did not speak, he went on, 'If I crossed to the same roof, Emmanuelle, both our names would be mud.'

'Yours already is,' Manny reminded him bluntly, and was maliciously pleased to see him wince.

'Yes,' he agreed, 'I'm not exactly a popular employer, am I? What would you suggest?'

'First of all your return to good health, for only then can you tackle whatever has occurred.'

'Unpopularity has.'

Manny agreed with him, then said tentatively: 'You're not being looked after over here, Huw—your doing or theirs, I don't know.'

'Mine,' Huw accepted. 'When I was asked if I needed assistance I proudly said no. You would have done the same.'

'Not if I needed help.'

'Well, *I* said it.'

'I can believe that. Look at you, half fed, half tended, even half bathed!'

'You plan to right all this? I would appreciate the last, I can't reach my back.'

Manny reddened. 'I plan to make you more comfortable than you are now.'

'The answer is thank you but no. I have a particular reason for remaining here, otherwise I would voluntarily go into hospital. But there's something going on somewhere and I have to be on hand.'

'I'm glad you said hand, because your leg's apparently of little help!' snapped Manny, irritated.

'Well, at least I can watch,' he replied dourly.

'You could watch at the cottage. We'd put you in the front room.'

'We?'

'Actually it was your niece who suggested all this.'

'I see.' His voice was dry.

'Will you come?'

'No. You know the way the talk would go.'

'According to you it's gone that way already.'

'Of course it has.' He permitted a brief grin. 'Men will be men.—Except, Manny, that I *wasn't*, was I?'

'Wasn't? Wasn't what?'

'A man.' He looked deliberately at her. 'I mean, Emmanuelle Norbert, if it had been Welsh——'

'Mr Grant, your niece—and I—think you should finish your convalescence away from here. Will you, or not?' Manny tacked on, a little shrilly: 'Jane will want to know.'

'Then tell Jane I decline with thanks. Tell her I shall stay here.'

'But——'

'Tell her I appreciate the thought. Then close the door as you leave.'

'But——'

He waved his arm, and, fuming, Manny went.

When Jane came home from school, Manny promptly told her, 'Your uncle is impossible! He won't come.'

'You asked him, Manny?'

'How otherwise would I know he won't come?' Manny snapped. She looked apologetically at Jane. 'He's difficult, to say the least.'

'All the family is,' shrugged Jane. 'It wasn't only Judy.'

'Well, we've done what we can. Of all the pig-headed——'

'Yes,' Jane agreed. She gave the impression of having cares of her own, so Manny left her on her own.

Manny found she had little inclination to work. When Jane went to her room to do her homework, an opportunity Manny always took to take stock of her day's painting, instead she put her brushes down and went to stand at the window. She frowned as she played with the blind cord, since, for all her dismissal of Jane's uncle to Jane, Manny could not quite dismiss Huw to herself. He had looked ill, she thought, very ill.

She looked across to the works. It was near-dark now, no outlines of buildings any more, only lights showing. As she watched a door under one of the lights opened and someone came out. For a moment he stood in the glow, and she saw it was Larry. She saw that he was crossing from the works to the cottage.

She went out to the verandah, her heart quickening.

Before Larry reached her Manny called: 'Larry, is it——'

'Yes, it's Grant. He's no good, Manny. Reckon it

cost him the world to tell me, but he sent Gerry over
to say I'd better get the doc.'

'And did you?'

'He's not there.' Elkington had only one doctor.
'There's been a major accident on the highway, and
all hands have been called in. But I described his
condition to his wife.'

'Yes, Esme was a nursing Sister.'

'And she said he was running a temperature. She
said it has to be brought down. While I bring him
over you get on to her.'

'But you mustn't move him, not now.'

'He's moved already.' Larry nodded to the works
where a posse of men were bringing Huw across.
'That's no place to be sick. You get a room ready,
a bed. Then get on the phone. Do what the doc's
wife says.' Larry paused. 'I'll help.'

Manny nodded. She turned and went into the
house, calling Jane as she went.

Jane sprang into immediate action, making Manny
sincerely believe that the girl was right in her nursing ambitions. She got to the other side of the bed
and together they made it. By the time they had
done, the patient had arrived, and one look at him
sent Manny racing to the phone.

By her side Jane said: 'I've taken his temperature,
Manny, and it's a hundred and three, and that's
onset of fever in my medical book. Tell Mrs Javes
that. Ask her what we have to do.'

Esme Javes came comfortingly back over the receiver that Manny and Jane shared anxiously.

'Don't panic over the temperature, onset of fever

is generally sudden. Open all the windows immediately and reduce that formidable pile of blankets I'm sure you have shoved on. One sheet will do.'

As Jane ran to comply Manny said doubtfully: 'It's not a hot night, Esme.'

'But *he* is,' Esme came in.

'In fact,' persisted Manny, 'it's slightly chilly. He could get pneumonia.'

'One sheet.' Esme's voice was crisp. 'His temperature, if it's what you say——'

Jane broke in with: 'Yes, Sister, it is.'

'—has to be reduced without delay. Harry would do that if he could come out, so you must believe me.'

'Oh, we do,' the girls assured her.

'Then spring into action,' Esme urged. 'The patient must be sponged at once. Then when he's finished, he must be sponged again. And again. Make the water around eighty-five degrees to begin with, then reduce it gradually. If it doesn't bring him down you'll have to begin cold packs.'

'I know about cold packs,' Jane claimed.

'Also he must drink copiously, cool lemonade would do fine. As much as he can swallow and more.'

'What else?' Manny asked.

'What else?' Esme sounded wryly amused. 'My dear Manny, you start doing that now, then you do it all night, then all day tomorrow if it still doesn't work. And you ask me what else? Now put down the phone and get going . . . and Manny, good luck.'

Esme's receiver was replaced, and, a little uncertainly, Manny did the same.

There was nothing uncertain about Jane, though.

Aided by Larry she was soaking sheets in cold water and wringing them out again, Larry one end, Jane the other. Larry crossed and lifted Huw up from the bed while Jane and Manny put the wrung-out sheet down, and then, after Huw was placed back again, a wrung-out top sheet was applied. Larry supported Huw while he was urged to drink, then it was time to do the whole thing from the beginning again.

'In my medical book,' said Jane, working on her side of the beetroot-red Huw, 'you keep a chart marked Tertian, Quartan, Remittent. Then there's a peak, and it's called Efflorescence, and it's either the turning point or not at all.'

'And it's here now, I'd say,' broke in Larry dramatically. 'The boss looks about to go up in fire.'

Manny looked at Huw, heard the hot gasps, saw his awful distress, and then, as she watched, as they all watched, the beetroot look began to pinken instead, and, putting her hand to Huw's face, Manny actually felt a first cooler touch.

'He's coming through,' she called.

'I think you're right, young Manny.' Larry was peering closely at Huw.

But Jane was making certain with the thermometer.

'He's dropping,' she triumphed, 'Uncle Huw's dropping!'

They looked across at each other and smiled.

From the bed Huw gave an exhausted but definitely alive groan.

CHAPTER THIRTEEN

DOCTOR JAVES arrived an hour later, and by that time Huw, less exhausted, was sitting up in bed and begging plaintively for sustenance, for something to eat, not drink.

Seeing the doctor, he appealed: 'Help me. I'm waterlogged.'

'Lemonade-logged,' corrected his niece.

'I want something solid. Tell these clots it's all right to cook me a steak.'

'Very efficient clots by the look of you,' the doctor praised, 'and I'd make that steak a poached egg. You can start serious refuelling in the morning. Do you hear that, girls? It will be quite safe to serve something more substantial then.'

'They won't be doing the serving,' Huw declared, 'I'll be back at the works.'

'Oh, no, you won't, you'll stay here.'

'But why? What's wrong? You just said——'

'That you look recovered? You do. But what made you descend to the depths of needing recovery in the first place, Huw? Simply this: You haven't been looking after yourself.'—Jane gave Manny an I-told-you look.—'I have no doubt you skipped your meals rather than drag yourself to the door to collect them, and consequently you reached a low ebb. This resulted.' The doctor nodded to the sickbed. 'Only through very good nursing have you come through

unscathed. Instead of complaining you should be
tendering your thanks.'

'Thank your wife very much,' said Huw. 'I'm told
she gave the instructions.'

'Quite easy on the other end of a wire,' said the
doctor drily. 'Carrying them out is the hard part.'

'Then thanks all round.' Huw's glance took in
Larry standing at the door. *'Thank you,'* he said
again.

Larry gave a wry look, then shrugged and went
away. After he had gone Huw turned to the doctor.

'I'd be all right over at the camp. The cook's first
class.'

'But no one actually brings your food to you, do
they?'

'To the door, as you just said, but how' ... Huw
frowned ... 'do you know?'

'Soleil Bay is Elkington's only project, so of course
we get to know.'

'No doubt then you also know that things are not
going as smoothly as they should of late?'

Doctor Javes nodded. 'Yes, we know that, too.'

'In which case I just have to be on hand.'

'So you will—but across the road. Sorry, Huw,
those are my orders for the next week. Now let me
look at that leg.'

He did so, said it was progressing favourably, then
extracted an unwilling promise from Huw not to
move until he checked again.

Jane had made tea, and they all sat round the bed
and drank it. Doctor Javes reported that the highway
accident had not been fatal but certainly messy. The

casualties had been sent by ambulance to neighbouring Glenville.

'We'll simply have to wangle a clinic here,' he hoped.

'I'll be the first nurse,' Jane declared.

'In your showing tonight I'll second that,' praised Doctor Javes. 'What about you, Manny?' He looked across Huw's sickbed to her.

'I'll be gone,' Manny answered.

'You think we'll take that long to get our hospital?'

'I trust not, but I'll be gone quite soon. I'm nearly up to my final mural panel, and after that I leave.'

There was a silence. No one broke it. At last Doctor Javes got up and said he must be going.

'You'll spare me a lot of trouble, Huw,' were his final words, 'if you do what I say.'

Huw grimaced, but did not disagree.

Jane, full of hospital talk, saw the doctor out. After they had left Huw said to Manny: 'What's this about you going away?'

'Of course I'll be going away. When my work is finished, I'm finished.' Before he could interrupt she added: 'Anyway, you show no great enthusiasm for the place. I never saw such a face as when you were ordered to stay put. Is Soleil that bad, then?'

'I never said so.'

'Your grimace did.'

'Then not for the reason you're thinking. No, it's because I'm having trouble, because I need to be constantly on hand to watch.'

'Isn't the word spy?' she corrected.

'Use whatever word you like, but there's someone over there undermining me. I have to find out and remove the rotten apple. Until I do we'll never have a good team.'

'Couldn't you be imagining it?' she asked.

'With tampered books? With important reports gone? In several instances rival firms beating me to permits to mine locations I'm sure they couldn't have known about before I knew?'

'But does it have to be an inside job?' Manny was thinking about the *un*locked door.

'Presumably it has to, now that I've restricted coming and going.'

'But——' But Manny did not tell Huw, she considered he had enough on his plate just now.

Huw *actually* had enough on his plate in the week that followed. In the way fever often works he came out of his pyrexia as good and even better than before, and his appetite was huge.

'Home cooking after project cooking is sheer bliss,' he said, wolfing a second slice of pie.

'Your own Cooky is an excellent chef,' Manny stated.

'But he doesn't wear a pink apron,' Huw grinned.

Manny flushed. She had stood in front of the mirror this morning deciding between pink and blue pinafores, and that grin made her suspect that Huw knew.

'I have work to do,' she said hurriedly.

'But I'm already washed and fed,' he pointed out.

'Work of *my own*. I'm finishing the second panel.'

'Then I'll come and watch you do it.'

'You should stay where you are, rest your leg.'

'I'll rest it as I watch you, Emmanuelle. I can either be assisted to the studio or I'll hobble. Take your pick.' He waited for her.

'Hobble,' said Manny heartlessly, starting down the hall. 'Anyway,' she called over her shoulder, 'how can you watch your team when you're watching me?'

'It's not during the day that things happen,' he sighed, and Manny felt a guilty burn for not having told him about the gate.

'You're red,' he pounced, 'almost as though you've been helping me instead of leaving me to limp along on my own. Don't tell me you're sickening.'

'I'm feeling quite normal, thank you.' Manny crossed to the studio and he dragged himself behind her. He sat at the window where he could observe the works, but every time Manny looked up he was observing her. She flushed a deeper pink.

'Are you sure you're all right?' he asked. 'Not worried? Apprehensive?'

'*Normal!*' he snapped.

But that evening Manny was not normal. She had never returned the key Huw had given her when she had asked permission to enter the works for sketching purposes. She had intended to, but she had not, and Huw had never requested it of her. Now, for some obscure reason thinking of the key, she looked where she always hung it, and it was not there.

She sat very still, trying to think back. It was no use, she had no ideas at all.

Jane was making her own way home from school right to the door these days. Manny would have questioned this, but Jane had forestalled any questioning by getting her uncle's support.

'It will do her good to walk the few miles from the bus,' Huw had told Manny.

... *What* bus? Then came at once to Manny's suspicious mind. But she did not pursue it, for the missing key was taking all her attention. Where was the key? Did its absence mean anything? Why wasn't it there?

At supper, Huw back in bed again after a day sitting up, as ordered by Doctor Javes, Manny said: 'Jane, do you remember a key I used to hang on the hallstand?'

'No ... no, I don't think I do, Manny. Would you prefer plain omelette or cheese?'

'All your omelettes are good, dear. Oh, drat the thing, I just don't know where I've put it.'

'... The key?'

'Yes.'

'Has Uncle Huw asked for it, then?' Jane's attention was on the omelette pan and the tricky business of turning the omelettes.

'No, but I said I would return it as soon as I needed it no longer, and I don't need it now. Besides——'

Jane's eyes flashed up from the pan, but Manny did not notice.

'Besides, Manny?' Jane asked.

'Well, the morning I came from the headland to alert the gang that Huw was injured the side entrance was unlocked. I only discovered it by accident, I gave it a casual push and then found I could get in. When

I mentioned it to Les later he said it was impossible, but' ... a shrug ... 'I was still there.'

'Oh,' was all Jane said. Presently she added: 'It wouldn't be important, though, would it? The—gate, I mean.'

'It, and the main gate, are the only ways to enter the works, that is unless you come in by helicopter, or fetch along a very high ladder, or don't mind scraping over barbed wire.'

'I meant it wouldn't be important to get inside, Manny. I mean, there's only big machinery that you couldn't possibly move, anyway. Nothing to—well, steal.'

'Steal?' queried Manny.

'I mean take.'

'Money left around, Jane? Money from pockets? Men in projects are very trusting.'

'Oh, but he wouldn't do that, I—I mean, no one would take such a trouble to get into—— Well, they would only be petty amounts.'

'Not always so petty. Also the office carries future plans, and they could be important.'

This time Jane said nothing. She took the dishes to the sink, then brought out the dessert.

'Will you take in Uncle Huw's?' she asked Manny.

'But you always do,' said Manny in surprise, for Jane, as hungry for praise as she was for everything else, always liked to be there at the first judicious bite.

'Please take it in,' Jane begged in a stifled kind of voice.

Manny looked at her puzzled.

'Jane, why don't you come home in the school bus any more?' she asked directly.

'Manny, please take in Huw's dessert.'

'Why, Jane? Why aren't you taking it in? Are you afraid your uncle will ask you that question as well?'

'Oh, Manny, *please*!'

After a moment, looking at the unhappy young face, Manny did. When she returned to the kitchen Jane was waiting for her.

'I'm miserable, Manny,' she blurted, 'and I have to tell you.'

'Are you sure,' Manny asked with a premonition, 'it isn't *Huw* you should be telling?'

'That I don't want to see Julian any more, Manny?' Jane asked.

'Oh, it's *that*! Girl talk!' Manny said with vast relief. For a moment she had thought there was going to be something heavy.

She looked at Jane, tiresome, most often preposterous but absolutely lovable Jane, and would have laughed at her but that the pretty young face was so doleful.

'Julian has been driving me all the way out, Manny,' Jane blurted, 'I haven't been walking home at all. Also, as you just said, I haven't been catching the bus. Julian has been collecting me at Elkington, and we come out by a different route, then sit in his car and talk until it's time for you to get me, or, as it has been this last week, time for him to take me to our lane.'

'Go on, Jane.'

'At first it was fun ... and then——'

'Then?'

'Then,' cried Jane, 'I just didn't want to do it any more.'

There was a moment's silence. Taking a deep steadying breath, Manny asked: 'Do what, Jane? Did' ... a second pause ... 'did Julian do anything to you?'

'No, Manny.' Jane shook her head emphatically. 'I just didn't want him suddenly, and the realisation of my fickleness made me terribly ashamed. I'm Judy all over again, was what I thought. So——'

'So, Jane?' Manny asked quietly.

'So I did something he asked me because I felt guilty about him. Oh' ... looking at Manny's worried face ... 'it was really nothing.'

'Yet enough to trouble you, Jane?'

'My trouble is because I don't want to meet him again but know I'll have to. He'll be there.'

'Where?'

'Where we both go.'

'Then everything's simple,' said Manny. 'See him tomorrow and tell him.'

'He'll never agree.'

'He would have to, wouldn't he? If you say you won't, he can't make you.'

'He wouldn't listen. But' ... hopefully ... 'he would believe it if *you* told him.'

'I?'

'Yes, Manny.'

'But I don't even know him.'

'He knows you, from all that I've told him.'

'Then I still don't know him, because you've told

me nothing, except the usual dreamboat bit.' Manny's voice was severe.

'And now he's not that any more, not, anyway, to me. Oh, Manny, I'm so unhappy! I don't want to do the things I do, but' ... a sob ... 'I've done them.'

'*What things,* Jane?'

'Nothing, really,' Jane said again. She was quiet for a few moments. 'But I keep on wondering could it be important——'

'Could what be important?'

But Jane had gone quiet again. It was not the time to probe her, so Manny said soothingly: 'You're young, dear.'

'I know,' burst in Jane, 'and that's why I'm asking you to help me, asking you will you see him, tell him I don't want to—— Well, *tell* him, Manny.'

'Now, Jane, don't be silly. You're going to be a nurse one day and make decisions and carry them out yourself. Make this decision now, then carry it out. Besides——'

'Besides, Manny?'

'Besides, I've enough to do on my own account. Until your uncle leaves us I have to be on hand in the cottage. Also I have my final panel to do. Then' ... a sigh ... 'I can go.'

'Oh, no, Manny, no!'

'It has to be, Jane.' Manny said it in a decisions-made and carried-out tone as an example for Jane. She got up and put the desserts neither of them had touched in the refrigerator.

'Get your uncle's plates, Jane,' she directed, and

went down the passage to the sudio and firmly closed the door.

But once there she did not take up any brush. Instead she sat at the window and looked out at the darkling evening. She was thinking deeply. Even when the last shadow fell she did not put on the light.

Some time later, she could not have said when, Manny fell asleep. She must have been mesmerised by the flickering stars, she thought, waking up later and stretching her chair-cramped limbs. It must be quite late, for the house was in darkness. She went quietly to the passage and saw that even Huw's light was out, and Huw always read until the small hours.

She came back to adjust the blind before she, too, went to bed, then, glancing across to the works, she stiffened. The moon had come briefly out of a cloud and it lit up the scene, and there at the works' side gate was the figure of a man. Without waiting a moment, without thinking what a foolish thing she could be doing, Manny ran out of the studio and across the road. She ran so fast he was still there when she arrived, then, looking at him, she knew why. Huw could not possibly get away in a hurry, not with his injured leg.

'Manny!' he exclaimed in complete surprise. 'Are you quite mad?'

'I saw you and I thought you were the fellow who'd been getting in ... or so you said.' Manny's eyes were on his dressing gown. '*You*'re the mad one,' she exploded, 'you'll have pneumonia.'

He ignored her. 'So you raced over, not thinking

what you might encounter. I could beat you for that, you reckless little idiot, except—except I'm kissing you instead.' He limped over, pulled her to him, and did.

Manny did not respond, the memory of her last response was still too clear in her mind. She had turned to him that time, she remembered, and given him back kiss for kiss. Her cheeks burned. If he reminded her of that now . . .

But Huw didn't. Instead he held her at arm's length a long moment.

'I can wait,' he said.

But he kissed her again, and this time he held the kiss.

'We'd better get back to the cottage.' His voice was gruff.

'Was the gate unlocked?' Manny asked as they started off.

'No, not tonight.'

'Not tonight? You mean, you've been checking it before?'

'Every night that I've been in your care.'

'And I had to answer to Doctor Javes for you!' Manny exclaimed indignantly.

'Yes, Manny, and I'm sorry about that, but it had to be done. I have to get this thing clear, otherwise you and I will never—will never——' He stopped suddenly and looked down at her. 'Manny,' he said unexpectedly, 'is *he* still there?'

'He?' Manny was bewildered.

'Welsh. Is he? Is he still in that funny little heart of yours?—— But don't tell me now. Just help me over this rough bit, because I can't afford to crack up at this stage. I'm going back to the works tomorrow, I have something to do, and neither you nor Javes can stop me.'

'Yes, Huw,' said Manny. She could have added:

'And I have something to do, too.'

For in her moments of deep thinking just before sleep had taken her something had struck Manny. It was possibly wrong, probably wrong, but still it had persisted, and she had decided that at the very least she must find out.

She was going to see this Julian of Jane's tomorrow, tell him what needed to be told ... and at the same time satisfy a suspicion that was growing stronger in her every minute.

When they reached the cottage Manny opened the door and held it while Huw hobbled in. She shut it after he went through, then helped him down to his room.

But at once she left him and hurried away. It was because his last kiss, that holding kiss, was still on her lips, and she did not want him to see it there, as she felt he must see it, still on her lips ... *waiting for more.*

Because I love him, Manny knew.

I love Huw.

CHAPTER FOURTEEN

I LOVE him. I love Huw. Again and again Manny tasted those words, listened to them, felt the warmth of them touching her heart. She lay very still in her bed, almost frightened to move for fear she lost some of the ecstasy that suddenly had taken possession of her. Yet *sudden*? she asked herself. No, only this new realisation was that, for unconsciously, and she accepted it, she had known right from the start.

Her animosity whenever Huw had been present had really been self-protection, she admitted. Instinctively she had shrunk from Huw, afraid of being hurt. She had withdrawn in case Huw was cynically amused at what he sensed in her, even though she had been unaware of it herself. She had recoiled, feeling that Huw had nothing to give back to her.

Oh, he had *pretended* to have it, but Manny was not so naïve as to think he had meant one word.—'I have to learn how to reach you with him standing between us,' he had said.—'You're the loveliest and dearest.—I have to have that loveliest.—I have to have you.'

Words, words, words.

No, Manny thought, I've been at Soleil Bay too long for that, I know that one woman among many men automatically makes that one woman legitimate prey. I've been made love to a dozen times, and taken it as seriously as I must now take this man ... take Huw. She clenched her hands on that.

But all this did not alter the way she felt about him, and again in the darkness Manny whispered those three wonderful words.

I love Huw.

She had never loved Justin, her mind ran on. That renunciation in the Hotel Southerly had really been the culmination of all the unconscious doubts that had been building up in her ever since their Sydney encounter, an encounter that had gone to her head, not her heart as she had supposed. When she had met Justin, unwittingly she had been looking for an escape from a situation she had never know before, so could not understand. It had been the intrusion into her life of a man called Huw Grant. She had welcomed Justin as a bolthole from fallibility. She had built herself up to a state of falling in love ... but *she had not loved*. Not until now.

Now she forced herself to concentrate on Justin, Justin Welsh who was also ... and Manny felt quite sure of it ... Julian Winthrop.

She could not have said when the certainty had come to her, only that she *was* certain. It was common knowledge that people who changed their names invariably retained the same initials, a similar trend. So Justin: Julian. Welsh: Winthrop. J. W. The same man.

Also Jane's description tallied. Dishy ... Oh yes, Justin had been that. Smooth. Sophisticated. Worldly. Yes, yes and yes.

Next she examined Justin's reasons for returning here. The apparent one was Emmanuelle Norbert, for after all she had been his fiancée. But, and

Manny faced it, deep down inside her she had always sensed that Justin had never been so engrossed in her as obsessed by Huw Grant, that his triumph in Manny Norbert was nothing compared to his triumph in paying back, through Manny Norbert, some score against his boss. She had known it even in her pleasure at being courted that betrothal weekend, known but dismissed the thought.

No, Justin could not have come back just for her.

Then for Huw? she asked herself. For what he could extract from Huw through the works? Yes, *the works.*

The works kept nagging at Manny. Justin had been discharged because of some discrepancy, the details of which Huw had never revealed. She, and the men, had been indignant, but——

But could it all have been the truth, and as grave as Huw had implied?

Most of all was the business that was going on now, the spying as she contemptuously had called it, springing from Justin? Was that the reason he had come back? If so which of the men was aiding him from the inside? unlocking the gate?

... Or had he been given a key?

Now Manny sat upright in her bed. *Jane,* she thought.

She slept after that. She did not know how she slipped off with her mind reeling as it did, but she woke fresh and alert, and at once sought Jane out.

Jane, anything but fresh and alert, was still in bed, and she turned miserably to Manny when Manny came in with tea.

'I never slept all night, Manny. I feel awful. I think I'll stay at home today.'

'Yes, you will stay at home, Jane, but I won't.'

'What do you mean, Manny?' asked Jane.

'I'm going in to meet this Julian of yours.'

'*Not* mine,' said Jane hysterically, proving that she had been suffering a night of confliction, 'and I don't think he ever really wanted me. I think, Manny, he wanted you.'

'Me, Jane? He couldn't.'

'Well, he was always asking me about you, I used to get quite jealous. That, of course, was when I thought I liked him.'

'And now you don't.'

'No, Manny, I think I even hate him. Oh, Manny, I really am Judy.'

'You're yourself, Jane. No one is anyone else unless they intentionally try to make themselves that, and even then they're still not that person. You mustn't torture yourself over changing, everyone changes. But all the same why have you travelled such a complete circle, Jane?' Manny asked carefully. 'Why do you dislike him so much?'

Jane avoided Manny's searching look, but it was no use.

'Jane?' Manny insisted, and unhappily Jane complied.

'After a few trips home I decided I didn't like him after all, Manny. He was too old.'

'You preferred maturity before.'

'The next time I gave him a long look, and I could see he had a mean face.'

'Jane, tell me the truth, you're only edging around it.'

Jane looked at Manny, and her face crumpled. 'He kept asking questions.'

'What kind of questions?'

'About you. After I went off him I didn't mind that. But I did mind his questions about Uncle Huw.'

'Huw?' queried Manny.

'Yes.'

'What were they?'

'Works questions. Did we ever go over there? How did we get in? After that he became a spider and caught me in his web.'

'Jane, don't be dramatic!'

'It's true, Manny,' Jane insisted. 'I've done awful things because of him. He said if I didn't do what he asked he would go to Uncle Huw and tell him.'

'Tell what, Jane?'

'Tell him lies, because they were lies.' Jane bit down on her lip.

'But, darling, he couldn't, could he, when there was no foundation. For there wasn't, was there?' Manny watched the girl's face.

'No, there wasn't, but I was still afraid. He has such a way of talking and I thought that Uncle Huw ...' Now Jane turned her head away. 'So——'

'So?'

'So I did what he asked. I thought it was harmless. The way he explained it, it *was* harmless.'

'How did he put it, Jane?' asked Manny.

'It was quite simple, and rather touching in a way. He said he longed to see his mates. He worked at the project once, Manny, I thought you might have known him.'

'Go on, Jane.'

'He told me Uncle Huw had a down on him and refused to let him visit his old friends. I was quite angry at first about that. So he asked me was there a key about anywhere, as Uncle Huw had begun to lock everything up each night. I—I said there was. At the time I was still angry with Uncle Huw for victimising him.'

'So you gave the key to Julian?'

'Yes. I thought nothing about it ... well, not all that much ... until you asked me last night, then said it was serious, and then—— well, I did think. Oh, Manny!' Jane burst into tears. After a while she said: 'I can't face him. I'm frightened of him. Help me, Manny.'

'I'm going to, Janey. I'm going to see him.'

'Today?'

'Today. You must tell me where you meet him and I'll meet him instead. You can stay at home, Jane. There now.' She wiped the tears from the streaked face.

Presently Jane managed a wobbly grin.

To Manny's relief when she took a cup of tea to Huw's room, Huw was gone. Gone, too, were the clothes that one of the men had packed and brought over from the camp. So Huw had done what he said he would, Manny thought, taking the cup back. She was more determined than ever that she would do what she had said as well.

It seemed an interminably long day. Without Huw

to attend to Manny should have been able to get through more mural work, but when she took up her brushes she found no inclination to paint, especially with Jane's miserable young face watching her.

'Cheer up, Jane, he can't hurt you,' she said at last.

'Justin or Uncle Huw?'

'Neither, you silly child.'

'No, perhaps not. But it was you I was really thinking about, Manny. I'm beginning to wonder if I did the right thing telling you. I thought I'd feel relieved, but all I feel is this awful fear.'

'A nice cup of coffee would help,' Manny suggested. 'Will you make some?'

'With cinnamon toast?' Jane asked, instantly diverted, and went out.

When it came time to drive into Elkington to be at the spot where Jane met Julian each afternoon Manny left the house outwardly confident for Jane's benefit but inwardly very uneasy. Try as she might she had still reached no decision as to how to make her approach. Also she still did not know whether Julian was Justin. It seemed likely remembering those two quick glimpses she had had that day, but *was* he?

An hour later Manny at least settled that. Julian was indeed Justin.

Jane had told her where to go, what time to go there, but when it actually came to it Manny found herself shrinking back, unwilling to meet Julian if he was a stranger, not wanting to meet Justin again.

All the same she went, and she did.

Justin had not noticed her. How could he, she had concealed herself behind a shop door. For a moment, thankful for her anonymity, Manny instinctively started to back off. Then she remembered the situation, Huw's position, Jane's ... hers ... and stepped forward instead.

'Justin!' she called.

'Manny! Manny darling!' Tall, handsome, smiling, charming, Justin wheeled round and came across to her. 'At last!' he sighed, and adroitly edged Manny around a corner of the street. 'You've been terribly slow catching up, Manny,' he said accusingly, 'I thought you would guess it was not Julian weeks ago. If only you had I needn't have wasted so much time, gas and fascination on that silly kid.'

'You mean Jane?'

'Dear Manny, I haven't been entertaining a troupe of adolescents, only one. Yes, Jane.'

'If you'd wanted to see me——' Manny began.

'Wanted? What a pale word! I was going crazy for you.'

Manny ignored his interruption. 'Then why didn't you come out in the open and visit me?' she finished.

'With him there?' he demanded.

'If by him you mean Huw Grant——'

'I do.'

'Then he's at the works, not the cottage.'

Justin gave a soft, meaning laugh.

'A cottage,' he smiled, 'paid for by the same Huw Grant.'

'Oh, no, it's a lease. Dad took it out before he died. I mean——' Manny's voice ran out. She was recalling going into Elkington that day and telling the same to the owner of the cottage. She was recalling his surprised look. So the money had come from—— She became aware that Justin was watching her with amusement.

'*Not* Dad,' he said.

'Well, no matter, anyway.' Manny spoke quickly, not wanting to put an emphasis on it. 'You could still have come openly to me.'

'And risk being thrown into jail.'

'For what, Justin?'

'Nothing, Manny, nothing at all. He, Grant, manipulated it—bosses can do that. He let me off, though, but with a proviso. I was not to see you, otherwise I would be charged. As I didn't fancy being behind bars, I lay low,' Justin shrugged.

'Huw could still have found out. Jane might have said something.'

'But Jane didn't. Oh, no, I had that kid like that.' Justin held out his hand with the index and third finger fastened tightly. The fingers were nicotine-stained, and Manny felt herself withdraw.

He must have sensed her withdrawal. Quite harshly he repeated: 'Jane wouldn't tell.'

'She told me.'

'I wanted her to alert you, to bring you looking for me. But she would never tell him.'

'I wouldn't be so sure of that—you see, she now dislikes you, Justin.'

'I know she does, and I wasn't meaning a still tongue because of affection but because of fear. Jane is frightened of me, frightened of what I could say.'

'You could say nothing,' declared Manny.

He smiled pityingly at her. 'You call a friendship that went a long way beyond coffees and drives home nothing?'

'But it didn't.'

'No? Well, I admit it's open to argument, Jane's side, mine. But how do you think Jane's *school* would take it?'

'You mean—— you can't mean——'

'There's not a kid who takes the school bus home who doesn't know that Jane has given up travelling on it.' Justin paused. 'And who doesn't know why.'

'You—you're vile!' she cried.

'Oh, come, little Manny, we loved each other once. Remember?'

'No, I do not remember!'

'But we did. You couldn't wait to pursue the thing to the end. You can't deny it, can you? Didn't you turn up at the church?'

'I—I——'

'But it wasn't to be, was it? *He* saw to that. At least' ... looking hard at Manny and tilting one eyebrow, a habit of his, she recalled ... 'unless you still have the same ideas?'

Manny opened her mouth to deny that vehemently, to tell him again that he was vile. She closed her mouth. Then quietly and composedly, scarcely believing her self-control, she said: 'Well, it could be.'

A flicker of interest came into his eyes. He gave a low laugh.

'So *that's* how it is, Manny. Well, well, I did expect to have to adopt stronger methods, but I'm not against a more tender path.'

'What do you mean, Justin?' She willed her voice

not to crack from the hate she was feeling for him.

'I mean you and I against Huw Grant, I mean a *team*, Manny.'

'But Jane? Then she didn't ... you didn't ...'

'I never cared for puppy fat,' he drawled, and Manny knew she really did hate him.

'What is it you're after, Justin?' she asked carefully.

'First of all you, darling, to shatter him. He always had an eye for you, Manny, remember I told you that.'

'But I don't want him, I want——' She looked up at Justin, wondering if she could pull it off. She put everything in that look, and she could see him looking thoughtfully at her. Had it worked?

'Do you know, little Manny, I do believe you're still soft on Justin,' he said at last.

'Then what do we do? What we planned, but didn't do, before?'

'You'd like that? Wedding bells? Yes, *wife*, we will. But before we do ...'

Manny did not know how she was slipped into his car that was waiting at the curb, how far they drove before Justin pulled into a quiet lane to tell her the rest.

'I'm on to a good thing, Manny,' he grinned. 'Another day and I would have been set. Only Jane, the young fool, evidently got scared. She never said she was backing out when I drove her home yesterday, but I could see the signs. When I saw you just now I thought it was all up, that he was close behind. Not for a moment' ... touching Manny's knee ... 'did

I dream you would still feel like you did.'

'That good thing you're on to, Justin?' Manny prompted.

'The mine. I'm being paid very handsomely for— information.'

'Information that you've stolen from——' Manny could have bitten out her tongue. Hopefully she summoned up an excited giggle. 'You're clever, Justin,' she awarded.

The praise disarmed him. He grinned crookedly and let his hand rest again on her knee.

'I'm bowing out tomorrow after this last look at what Grant is on to,' he said.

'Rutile?'

'Dear little idiot, *apparently* it's that, but I can tell you it's *much, much more.*'

'Then tell me, Justin.'

He smiled and shook his head. 'I won't even tell my wife until it's done. But I promise you that then we'll both laugh over it, laugh over what its loss ... *and the loss of Manny Norbert* ... will do to King Grant.'

'You hate him, don't you, Justin?' she said quietly.

'I love you,' he answered, and the hand on her knee pressed down.

'I'll want you to help me, Manny,' he told her. 'I'm not quite sure about Jane, for all that I said I had her like that.' Again he snapped his fingers. 'I want you to watch her end.'

'Until you—— until we——'

'Until we get away,' he confirmed.

'When will that be?'

'After I conclude this business at the works' ... a pause ... 'collect you.'

'Collect me where?' Manny asked.

'At the end of your track. That's where I leave the car.'

'What time?'

'Dark.'

'Can't you get nearer than that?'

'Darling girl, you won't be kept waiting,' he assured her.

'So I keep an eye on Jane, and then——'

'Yes, Manny. After that——' He put his arm round her waist.

Manny nodded dumbly, afraid to speak for fear her excitement showed. He was actually believing her, she thought.

'I'll get you back now,' he said presently. 'Do nothing. Say nothing. That's my Manny.'

... Is it? thought Manny.

Her excitement was near fever-pitch now and she was finding it difficult to keep calm. In his absorption she saw that Justin had not noticed that his wallet had slipped from his hip pocket and now rested between their two seats. She could see the glint of a key, and at once recognised it. It was the same key that had hung in the hall but wasn't hanging there any longer. Huw's gate key. The key that Jane had given to Justin. As he reversed the car out of the lane Manny removed the key, and as he started along the road again she slipped it into her bag.

He was driving in his usual relaxed fashion, and Manny let his hand rest on her knee until he put her off at the track.

'Goodbye, Mrs Welsh,' he grinned.

'Goodbye, Justin.'

'You know the drill?'

'Of course.' Manny stepped out of the car and hurried down the path.

It was rather an anticlimax when she entered the house to find Jane stirring something at the stove, too intent on whatever she was concocting to look up as she greeted Manny with a casual: 'Hi.'

Manny waited for an anxious enquiry as to how things had gone, but Jane kept stirring, and presently, rather piqued, Manny proffered:

'All's well, Jane, you can stop worrying.'

Jane looked up now, but only briefly. 'I knew you'd fix things, Manny,' she smiled.

It was acknowledgment, Manny supposed, but still a letdown. She said: 'Hold off supper, Jane. I have to see Huw.'

'He's not there.'

'He must be there,' Manny protested, trying not to betray her anxiety. She had to see Huw at once, tell him, alert him. It was imperative. 'He must be there,' she repeated, 'I mean, he can't get around without help, so how could he be gone?'

'I don't know, Manny, all I can tell you is that he rang me to say he would be away should anyone want to see him.'

Want to see him! Manny bit her lip.

'Then I'll go over and see Larry,' she tried next.

'Everything is locked up over there. I was standing at the window when they did it.'

'Then I'll ring Larry to let me in.'

'He's not there either, Manny, he went with Huw.'

'With Huw?' echoed Manny.

'Yes. Besides——'

'Oh, what else, Jane?' Manny demanded angrily.

'Besides, the phone is out of order. You can't ring.'

'It can't be. It was all right this morning.'

Jane hunched her shoulders, and Manny went into the passage to take up the receiver. But she did not reach the telephone. She turned back, aroused by an unusual noise.

'Jane——!' she called. It had almost sounded like a scuffle. 'Jane, what is it?'

Then she stopped.

Jane had been impelled to the door leading from the kitchen to the hallway. Behind her, his hand lightly but meaningfully on her shoulder, stood Justin Welsh.

CHAPTER FIFTEEN

THE first thing that struck Manny was Jane's composure. For a girl who had cried out her fear, who had begged for help, Jane was very much in control of herself.

The second thing to strike home was Justin's duplicity. Not for one moment had she really deceived Justin, Manny realised. Where she had thought she had been clever, *he* had been the clever one, letting her believe that.

He was smiling meanly now, and approaching her,

bringing Jane with him, his hand still lightly yet intentionally on the girl's shoulder.

'The key, Manny,' he told Manny, 'I want the key you took. Oh, yes, I saw you do it. I intended it like that. Why otherwise did I let my wallet slip down, you little fool? Not for a moment did you put it over me, I've had more than my share of big eyes and innocent looks. So I gave you full rope to make sure of you, whether you were genuine or acting a part.' Another mean smile. 'You pulled the rope too far. Now, the key, Manny.'

'I—I gave it to Huw,' Manny said desperately.

'Grant's not here, and hasn't been all day. He won't be back until late—I checked that out earlier. I always check. I have a way.' Another mean smile. 'Now think up another one.'

'Larry has the key, I gave it to him.' Manny knew she was talking wildly, but still did not stop herself. If nothing else she could be gaining time, she hoped.

But Justin disallowed that time. Still holding Jane, he came right up to Manny.

'*You* have it. Not Grant or Larry. The day those two come together is very far off.'

'... Not so far off, Welsh.' The voice came from the other end of the hall.

Manny turned, not believing what she heard. Justin wheeled round and Jane stepped promptly away.

Huw came right into the corridor.

'You——' Justin muttered thickly.

'And me.' Larry was close behind Huw.

'*Not* so far off, Welsh,' Huw said again. 'To date our only real contact is a fellow-dislike of Justin

Welsh, but it's a fair enough start. What do you say, Larry?'

Larry nodded briefly to Huw, then gave his attention to Justin.

'You went too far, Welsh,' he said with contempt. 'Company spying might pass me by, I don't understand these things, but when it comes to taking from your mates . . .'

'I didn't!'

'You were *seen*. One of the fellows who had found his pockets lighter stayed up one night to satisfy himself. What can you answer to that?'

'I was down to the bone,' Justin pleaded. 'I had to live. Don't forget I'd been unfairly discharged.'

'I thought so at the time. I was on your side. But when it came to stealing from your mates . . .'

'I never did.' Justin tried that again.

'Man, you were *seen*.' Larry's voice held utter disgust. 'You were after big fish, but you couldn't resist the small sprat. Perhaps I could understand robbery, but pilfering? Pah!' He turned to Huw. 'It's your go now. Do you want me to wait with you, boss?'

'With *this*?' If Larry's voice had held disgust, Huw's voice held loathing. 'No, I'll manage. But thanks, Larry.'

'Just make those thanks an open gate again,' Larry grinned. 'Allow us coats flung over chairs again. A full swear tin, not a pilfered one.' He gave Justin a last withering look and went.

As the door slammed, Huw turned to Justin.

'You can go next. I'm preferring no charges for the paltry amounts your paltry nature has urged you to take, and as for the other, Larry's big fish ... well, what you believed you could sell doesn't stand any more. To be brief, your intending receivers have had a compulsory change of mind. I'd keep clear of them if I were you.'

He came right up to Justin now.

'Because of my sister, because of what you must have meant to her once, I'm letting you go. But by God, if you ever come round again, come near—my wife ...' He turned now and looked fully at Manny.

Something stirred in Manny, something as elemental as life itself. She moved quickly to stand beside Huw.

'Go, Welsh,' Huw said thickly, 'and never come again, or by heaven——'

Without a second look, Justin went.

It was a long five minutes before Manny realised that Larry had left, that Justin had, that Jane had slipped out. That only she and Huw remained.

She was still standing beside him, but, and she could not have said why, she moved away from him and looked across at him from the other side of the room.

'Huw?' she asked.

His silver eyes met and held hers, but he did not move across to be with her.

'Judy was my baby sister,' he said. 'Jane's mother was the firstborn, then I came, then, years after, Judy.

'How can I describe her, Manny? Birds singing? Rainbows after a storm? Sunshine? Spring? Anyway, all the family knew it, loved her for it, cherished her more, I suppose, than she deserved. Oh, yes, Judy was spoiled. But she was still our Judy, impressionable, irresponsible ... rash.'

'Yes, Jane said that.'

He nodded and grew silent.

After a while Manny broke the silence.

'Jane also said that Judy went away and no one knew where.'

'I know now. Welsh told me when I took over. He shrugged as he said it.' Huw clenched his hands. 'She went away with him.'

'And never told you?'

'*How could she?*'

'You mean——'

'... Yes, I mean that she—died.'

'But——' Manny began.

'Oh, I know it can't happen, people don't die of broken hearts, but that child did.'

'She'd married him?'

'Oh, no, he doesn't deal in marriage, not our Welsh. He wouldn't have married you, either, when it came to it.' Now Huw began pacing the room.

'As I told you, Welsh was already here when I took over, in fact it was because of him I was sent. Very soon after his own arrival Welsh had gathered that it was more than rutile that was being mined. Since old Peter, at the end of his term, couldn't handle it, I was called upon to trouble-shoot.

'My appointment here was a shock to Welsh, and he would have got out at once, but he'd committed himself by peddling future sources. He lay low for a while, but I wanted him right away immediately, I couldn't stand him around, so when the discrepancy occurred I gave him no second chance.'

'You'd known Judy had gone away with him?'

'I'd suspected it,' Huw said, 'and when I fired Welsh my suspicions were confirmed. He told me. He also told me—the other.'

There was silence again.

'The things I said to Welsh that day,' Huw resumed, 'would have sent any other man to the ends of the earth. But Welsh came back.'

'Not for me,' Manny said urgently.

'Oh, I know that. I knew the only reason was to get what he came for in the first place.'

'Money?'

'What else?'

'You knew he was around, Huw?'

'I knew it.' The silver eyes flicked at Manny.

'However, he's history now as regards the company, and any other company I can persuade. Welsh will never work on any other project if I can help it. Also our men here, every one of them, are applauding me. He's finished, just as he finished my sister when she was little more than a girl, scarcely older than Jane.'

'Jane,' remembered Manny, 'was very controlled tonight.'

'Of course. She knew Larry and I were waiting in the studio, had stood there the last hour.'

'You expected something like this?' she asked.

'Sooner or later, Manny.'

'Did you order Larry to be there?'

'Order him? Larry would have attended to Welsh

in his own way had I not been there to stop him.
Larry doesn't understand my side of the business, and
I don't think he wants to, but he does understand
fingers on other people's property.' Huw gave a short
bitter laugh.

'Three questions,' said Manny.

'Yes?' He had not attempted to cross to her after
she had moved away.

'Jane? Is Jane your sister Judy again?'

'No.' He permitted a smile. 'Jane is Nurse Jane.
Very definitely Nurse Jane. What do you think?'

'Sister Jane,' Manny promoted. She permitted a
smile back.

'Second question?' he prompted.

'The cottage ... Dad never leased it, did he?
You did.'

'Yes. I had to, Emmanuelle, to answer your third
question.' He waited.

'*Wife*,' he reminded her when she did not speak,
'as used in warning just now to Welsh. For you were
going to ask that, weren't you?'

Manny could find no words.

'You see, I knew you were going to be that right
from the beginning, but how in heaven could I con-
trive it if I let you get away? So——'

Now he was crossing to her at last, crossing slowly,
maddeningly slowly. Oh, Huw, hurry, hurry! her
heart called.

'From the first moment I saw you I was sure,
Manny. I knew it. I knew I had to make you know,
too. You don't know yet, but it will come. Manny, it
has to. Do you hear?'